The Magnificent Mulligans™

BOOK TWO

LIONS, ELEPHANTS, AND LIES

Bill Myers

Illustrations by Greg Hardin

FOCUS
ON THE FAMILY.

A Focus on the Family Resource
Published by Tyndale House Publishers

A Focus on the Family book published by Tyndale House Publishers, Carol Stream, Illinois 60188

Focus on the Family and the accompanying logo and design are federally registered trademarks, and *The Magnificent Mulligans* is a trademark, of Focus on the Family, 8605 Explorer Drive, Colorado Springs, CO 80920.

Tyndale and Tyndale's quill logo are registered trademarks of Tyndale House Ministries.

All Scripture quotations, unless otherwise marked, are from *The Holy Bible, English Standard Version.* Copyright © 2001 by CrosswayBibles, a publishing ministry of Good News Publishers. Used by permission. All rights reserved.

Scripture quotations marked (NIV) are taken from the *Holy Bible, New International Version*®, *NIV*®. Copyright © 1973, 1978, 1984, 2011 by Biblica, Inc.® Used by permission of Zondervan. All rights reserved worldwide. (www.zondervan.com) The "NIV" and "New International Version" are trademarks registered in the United States Patent and Trademark Office by Biblica, Inc.®

Cover and interior illustrations by Greg Hardin. Cover design by Michael Harrigan.

For Library of Congress Cataloging-in-Publication Data for this title, visit http://www.loc.gov/help/contact-general.html.

For manufacturing information regarding this product, please call 1-855-277-9400.

For information about special discounts for bulk purchases, please contact Tyndale House Publishers at csresponse@tyndale.com, or call 1-855-277-9400.

Printed in the United States of America

ISBN 978-1-64607-114-2

29	28	27	26	25	24	23
7	6	5	4	3	2	1

"The LORD detests lying lips,
but he delights in people who are trustworthy."

—PROVERBS 12:22, NIV

Table of Contents

1

Just for Starters

"YOU AIN'T NERVOUS, ARE YOU?"

"Me?" Lisa half swallowed, half squeaked. "What's to be nervous about? Flying six miles above the earth in a metal tube at five hundred miles per hour?"

Nick chuckled. "Yeah, first time flying can be a little crazy. But not if you're a seasoned pro."

"Like you, I suppose," she said.

"Of course." Nick gave a little yawn to prove his point.

Dad sat in the middle seat and turned to speak to Nick at the window seat. "You've done a lot of flying?"

"Sure," Nick said. "That time I flew from New York to start living with you all."

"And now you're a pro?" Lisa said.

"Well, yeah. With my superior intelligence and quick ability to adapt, you bet."

If Lisa rolled her eyes any harder, they would have stuck in the back of her head.

Nick leaned over Dad and waved to the passing flight attendant. "Ma'am?" he said. She came to a stop. "Can you get my little friend here some milk?"

"Nick," Lisa whispered. "I'm fine."

He ignored her and said to the attendant, "First time flyers—they can be such rookies."

"Nick—"

"Trust me," he said. "It calms the nerves, helps settle the queasy stomach."

"My stomach isn't—"

He turned back to the attendant, "Oh, and could I have another Diet Coke. It's still free, right?"

The attendant nodded. "One milk, and . . ." with a patient breath, she added, "*another* Diet Coke."

"And lighter on the ice this time." Looking toward Lisa, he explained, "Less ice means more soda. Another little tip I'm happy to share."

Lisa slumped into her seat and sighed. It was going to be a long trip, and not just because they were going to Africa.

Africa? "Why are they going to Africa?" you ask. And you are asking, right? (If not, this next paragraph is going to be real boring.)

Last week Dad got a call from the Botswana Wild Game Reserve. A newborn elephant's mother had died, and the baby elephant was so heartbroken that he wouldn't eat, drink, or do anything else to survive. Because we Mulligans have a reputation for helping animals, and because we solved a similar problem with Gus, our own young elephant, the Botswana staff called us. And since Mom and Dad have this policy to always say yes to folks, they agreed. Of course, everyone— including a certain cute chimpanzee (that's me!)—wanted to go along. But because Lisa has this cool way with animals, and because Nick is . . . well, Nick, they were the two who got to fly over there with Dad.

"Here you go," the attendant said, handing Lisa the small carton of milk and leaning over to hand Nick a Diet Coke.

"Great," he said. "And do you have any more pretzels?"

"Nick," Dad warned.

"Hey, I'm a growing boy."

"In both directions," Lisa said.

He looked down at his gut and immediately sucked it in.

Dad continued, "You've been eating junk food ever since we got on the plane."

"I'm fine," Nick said. He turned back to the attendant. "How about a couple more packs of peanuts?"

Before she could answer, the airplane gave a little

LURCH

"What was that?" Lisa asked in alarm.

The attendant smiled. "Just a little turbulence. Nothing to worry—"

She was interrupted by another and much bigger

LURCH

Suddenly, the overhead "Fasten Seat Belt" light came on.

"Dad . . ." Lisa said.

"We'll be fine," Dad said calmly. (He might have been more convincing if the flight attendant hadn't just dashed to her own seat to buckle in.)

And then, just to keep things interesting, the plane started to

BOUNCE . . . BOUNCE

and

BUCK

so much that Nick nearly spilled his soda.

"Whoa, that was close," he said as he took a big sip so he wouldn't lose any of the precious liquid.

"Are we going to be okay?" Lisa asked. There was no hiding the quaver in her voice as she reached for her seat belt.

"Sure we will," Nick said. "Nothing to worry about." But somehow he didn't sound quite as convincing as before. He turned to Dad who was fumbling for his own seat belt. "Right, Dad?"

Even though Dad is really Nick's uncle (long story that I'll bore you with some other time), he now calls him Dad like the rest of us.

BOUNCE . . . LURCH . . . BOUNCE

"Dad?"

BUCK . . . BUCK . . . BOUNCE

"Daaaaad? Is everything okay?"

LURCH . . . BOUNCE . . . LURCH

Things were a lot quieter in Mom's car as we all headed for school.

Not that I go to school.

(Not that I haven't tried.)

But the school officials are really prejudiced against so-called "nonhumans." And don't get me started on their dress code. They kept demanding I take off my fur coat, which as you might have guessed, I'm quite attached to.

Anyway, with Dad gone, Mom was pulling double duty, and we were all packed into her SUV tighter than pickles in a pickle jar.

In the far back, the twins, Jessica and Janelle, were carrying on a secret conversation that I'll tell you about later. In the next seat up sat Hector, the ten-year-old tough guy from Colombia. Tough except when it came to little Julie and Alan, the baby who sat in the car seat beside him. Around those two, Mr. Tough-as-Nails always became Mr. Jell-O-Pudding.

And up front sat me and my best pal, Stephie. Me because

Mom needed someone mature and intelligent to keep her company and Stephie because my friend was having a hard time not going to Africa with Dad.

"I never get to do anything," she grumbled.

Mom smiled. "I can give you a few more chores if that helps."

"Very funny. I mean important stuff, like helping with the animals."

"You've got Winona."

I leaned against Stephie, batting my eyes and throwing in a little

OO-oo Ah-ah EE-ee

Unfortunately, that only earned me a little scratch behind the ears—not the banana I was hoping for, which I'd seen packed in her lunch bag. But that's okay. School was still nine minutes away. I had plenty of time to work my animal charm on her.

"It's my autism, isn't it?" Stephie complained. "You're afraid to give me responsibility because you don't think I can handle it."

"Sweetheart . . ."

Stephie bit her lip and looked out the window. Big tears welled up in her eyes.

Of course, then Mom went into Mom Mode—you know, saying how she and Dad loved Stephie just as she was, along with all the other stuff they teach you to say in Mom

School. And then she added, "You know, with Lisa gone, I bet Janelle could use some help reintroducing the lion cub back to Golda, his mother."

Stephie lit up. "Could I?"

Mom grinned. "Fine with me if it's fine with Janelle." Glancing into the mirror she called, "That okay with you, Janelle?"

"Yeah, sure, whatever," Janelle said as she continued listening to Jessica's plan. (I'll tell you about this soon, I promise.)

And me? I reached up and gave Stephie's cheek a big victory

SMOOCH!
(I told you I had charm)

and gave another

OO-oo Ah-ah EE-ee

for good measure—all the time keeping my eye on her lunch sack. One minute had already passed. But I still had eight to go.

It took half an hour for the plane to end its imitation of a roller coaster.

Dad glanced down to Lisa. "How you doing, kiddo?"

She nodded, her voice still a little shaky. "I'm good," she said.

Turning to Nick, he asked, "And you?"

But Nick wasn't talking. I guess it's hard to talk when

pretzels, peanuts, and Diet Cokes are trying to make a repeat appearance in your mouth.

"You don't look so good," Dad said.

"I . . . (*swallow*) um . . ." (*swallow, swallow*)

"You're white as a sheet."

"Um . . ." (*swallow, swallow*)

"Here." Dad dug into the seat pocket and pulled out an air sickness bag.

Nick shook his head.

"You sure?"

"Those things are for wimps. I'm (*swallow*) fine."

"If you say so."

"Yeah, I—" A strange look came over Nick's face. Without a word, he unbuckled his seat belt and stood up.

"Nick!" Lisa complained. "What are you—"

"Restroom!" he blurted as he crawled over Dad and then Lisa.

"Doesn't exactly look 'fine' to me," Dad said.

Once he was standing in the aisle, Nick patted his hair into place and calmly replied, "As I said, I'm perfectly—"

Suddenly, his eyes widened. Throwing both hands over his mouth, he made a mad dash for the restroom.

I'd like to say that he made it in time. I'd like to say that, but I can't. Instead, all I can say is

GROSS!

2

The Plan Hatches

"YOU CAN'T BE SERIOUS," JANELLE WHISPERED as they headed down the middle school hallway.

"Why not?" Jessica said. "We're identical twins. Well, except for your glasses. But Mrs. Crawly won't know the difference."

"You really want me to go into your English class and do the spelling bee for you?" Janelle said.

"You're a brainiac. That's why they advanced you up a grade higher than me. You can do this bee in your sleep."

"I don't know."

"You be me and I'll be you," Jessica said. "Watch this." She grabbed Janelle's glasses and put them on. "Hi, my name is Janelle, and I'm so smart that I know the square root of 119 is . . . is . . ."

"10.9089," Janelle said. "When rounded up to the nearest fourth decimal."

"See," Jessica said. "A natural-born genius. Though you didn't hear that from me. I am, of course, still your sister."

"Of course," Janelle said. "What do I get out of the deal?"

"What do you want?"

Janelle frowned in thought. "Well, I hate gym class," she said. "Everyone makes fun of me."

"Because you're such a chicken—afraid of everything," Jessica said.

"Well, there is that."

"And you're so clumsy, you trip over your own shadow."

"And that."

"And you don't even know how to—"

"Okay, I get it," Janelle said.

"So . . . I'll take gym class for you. They're at the same time."

"You mean trade places?" Janelle asked.

"Exactly. You show everyone in English how smart I am, while I amaze everyone in your gym class so they'll stop teasing you."

Janelle frowned harder, trying to think of an excuse. "What about my glasses? I can't see without my—"

"So you trip over a desk or two. Big deal."

"It's just not right."

Jessica sighed. "Why are you always such a coward?"

"I hate doing wrong," Janelle said.

"So just pretend it's right."

"But it's *actually* wrong."

"You're right."

"I'm right?"

"Exactly! See how easy it is to pretend?"

"Jess, that's not how it works."

Jessica grinned. "You ever think about all those germs that creep around on the locker room floor?" she asked.

Janelle gave a shiver. As a world-class germophobe, the thought creeped her out. "Jess, don't—"

"And after gym class, as you're standing there in your bare feet, and you can feel them crawling right up your leg . . ."

"Jess—"

"Then up your body and onto your face."

"Jessica."

"And before you know it, they're climbing right inside your nose and—"

"Stop it!"

Jessica smiled. "So we have a deal?"

"I don't . . ."

"Well, if it isn't the mutant Mulligans," a girl's voice called out.

The twins turned to see Chloe and her clones approach. Pretty, rich, and popular, Chloe was the snobbiest girl in school. Seriously, she walks with her nose so high in the air, folks wonder why it doesn't scrape the ceiling. And did I mention pretty? Anyway, because Jessica and Janelle refuse to join Chloe's wannabe fan club, they're at the top of her hit list.

Turning to Janelle, Chloe said, "So, Jessica, are you ready to get totally crushed in today's spelling bee?"

"I'm not Jessica," Janelle said. She started to push up her glasses then realized her sister was still wearing them.

"Right," Chloe snickered. "How stupid do you think I am?"

"How many ways are there?" Jessica said, pushing Janelle's glasses up on her nose.

Chloe glared at Janelle. "I'm going to stomp you so hard, you won't even remember how to spell 'cat.'" Her followers giggled. "And just so you know, it's spelled with a '*c*' not a '*k*.'"

More giggles as Chloe flipped aside her perfect hair and headed down the hall. Her fan club turned to follow, flipping aside their own perfect hair.

Jessica leaned to Janelle and whispered, "See how easy it is? Nobody will ever know."

Chloe called back over her shoulder, "Oh, and Janelle? Congratulations on making it all the way to school without falling down."

Janelle bit her lip, but Chloe wasn't finished. "But be careful on those stairs. Raising one foot above the other can really get confusing."

As the Chloe fan club sauntered down the hall, Jessica saw Janelle's face grow hot with anger. She had Janelle just where she wanted her. "So what do you say? We put Chloe in her place, and I show your gym class you're a super jock?"

Janelle watched Chloe disappear around a corner.

"Well?"

Once again, Janelle reached to push up her glasses that were no longer there. Then, ever so slowly, Janelle began to nod. "Alright," she said. "But just this once."

"Absolutely!" Jessica said. She stuck out her hand to shake. "Just this once . . . Jessica."

"Wow, that's a lot of luggage for a little girl," Dr. Mooketsi joked. Dr. Mooketsi is the doctor from the Botswana Wild Game Reserve. He finished loading the van and helped Lisa inside with Nick and Dad.

"Actually," Dad said, "most of the stuff belongs to Nick."

"He likes variety," Lisa said. "Comes in handy with all the selfies he takes."

Instead of a witty comeback, Nick stayed slumped in the seat, looking whiter than frost on a snowbank in the middle of an Antarctic snowstorm. (Translation: He was still pale.)

As they drove off, Dad explained, "Our flight was not what Nick would call a good time."

Lisa giggled. "He hates roller coasters."

"Not to worry," Dr. Mooketsi said, chuckling. "A good night's rest and some delicious beans, porridge, and goat meat stew will make you better in no time."

Leaning over to Dad, Nick whispered, "Still got those air sickness bags?"

Meanwhile, Lisa was talking with Kelebogile, a Botswana girl about Lisa's age. The two were fast becoming friends. But it was difficult for Lisa to get a word in. Kelebogile ("Just call me Kele," she said) seemed to be an Olympic champion speed-talker.

"You'll just love it here in Botswana," Kele said.

"Great," Lisa said, "I—"

"Our headquarters aren't far from the Chobe River."

"Terrific, I—"

"That's where thousands of elephants come this time of year."

"Really? I—"

"But lots of elephants means lots of poachers."

"And—"

"The poachers kill the elephants just for their tusks. For the ivory. Isn't that sad? That's all they do. They just kill the elephants for their tusks and leave their bodies to rot."

"That's awful—"

"But my dad is going to stop them. That's why Dr. Mooketsi hired him, because he's really good at that. He's going to *stop* them, just you wait."

"And the baby eleph—"

"Thato, that's his name. He saw the whole thing. His mother getting killed, I mean. He won't eat or drink or do anything. It's like he wants to die. When my dad found Thato, he was lying beside his mother, actually crying. Thato, not my dad, though my dad can be an old softie too."

"Really crying?"

"Elephants have tons of emotions."

"I know, but—"

"So, are you really blind?"

"Yes, but I—"

"That must be terrible."

"Actually, it's—"

"That's probably why you're so good with animals."

"I don't—"

"Tomorrow morning, I'll show you around so you can see the place. Well, not *see*, sorry about that, but you'll just love it here in Botswana. Did I say that already? I forget. Sometimes I talk so much I don't even hear myself."

"Really?" Lisa said, pretending to be surprised.

"Yeah. That's why it's so great to have a friend my age to share stuff with. You know, someone to talk and listen to?"

Lisa nodded. She understood the listening part. But when it came to talking, well, it looked like that would be Kele's department.

3

The Lie Begins

"AND JESSICA," MRS. CRAWLY SAID, turning to Janelle. "Your word is: *deception*."

Janelle swallowed. She took a breath, then swallowed again. Not that there was anything left to swallow. Her mouth was drier than sand in a clothes dryer in the middle of the Sahara Desert . . . at high noon.

Translation: Her swallower had no swallowing left to swallow.

So there she stood with the rest of the class at the front of the room, staring back at Mrs. Crawly. At least she thought it was Mrs. Crawly. (It was hard to tell without her glasses.)

Now it was about to begin:

THE SPELLING SHOWDOWN . . .
down . . . down . . .
(that's supposed to be an echo)

Probably better known as:

THE GREAT LIE . . . ie . . . ie . . .
(another echo)

Could she really do this? Pretending to be Jessica wasn't *exactly* lying. No one *asked* her if she was Jessica—they just guessed she was.

(Not that it was a tough guess . . . with her carrying Jessica's books, sitting in Jessica's desk, and answering whenever anybody called Jessica's name.)

But was this truly not lying?

Or was it?

"Jess?" Mrs. Crawly repeated.

Janelle blinked, tried pushing up her glasses which were no longer there, and just because she was stubborn, tried swallowing again.

Earlier, right before class, she'd almost backed out. Standing outside the classroom, she had whispered to Jessica, "I can't do this."

Jessica, who now wore Janelle's glasses, said, "Yes you can. You *have* to. For both of us. To defend the Mulligan family honor."

"Actually, I don't think lying and cheating are how you defend—"

"So, are you ready for complete embarrassment?" a familiar voice said.

The twins turned to see Chloe and her fan club approach the room. As president of the club, Chloe gave her best fake smile (which in the Club Rulebook meant her best not-so-fake sneer). Obeying the rules, the others did the same.

Chloe continued, "Prepare for total humiliation."

Before Janelle could answer, Jessica shot back, "There'll be total humiliation, all right." She nodded toward Janelle. "But it won't be Jessica's."

Chloe turned to Jessica in surprise. "Well, look at this, girls. The cowardly Janelle can actually speak up." Cranking up her smile to *Ultra-Sneer*, Chloe flipped her hair to the side and entered the classroom . . . followed by her smiling, hair-flipping fans.

Janelle gritted her teeth. "*Cowardly?*"

Jessica grinned. "Not for long, sis. You're about to amaze them with *my* courage in your P.E. class. And I'm going to . . ." She waited until Janelle finally answered:

"You're going to crush them with *my* smarts in your English class."

"All right!" Jessica said as they fist bumped (which took a couple of tries before Janelle could finally see her sister's fist).

Then, taking a deep breath, she turned and boldly entered the room—though it might have come across as bolder if she hadn't run into

CLUNK

the edge of the door.

"Almost," Jessica whispered. She took her sister by the shoulders and moved her a little to the left. "There you go."

"Thanks," Janelle whispered.

Now, back in class, Mrs. Crawly asked for the third time. "Jessica? Do you or do you not know how to spell *deception*?"

Pushing up glasses that were still not there, and swallowing a mouthful of nothing that was still not there, Janelle finally answered: "Deception: D-e-c-e-p-t-i-o-n."

Gasps of surprise over "Jessica's" sudden intelligence filled the room.

Later in the day, after school let out, Stephie was helping Janelle with the baby lion.

Now, I want to make one thing perfectly clear: I was NOT jealous. I was still Stephie's best friend, so what's there to be jealous about?

So what if she was holding Bubba, the cute little lion cub, in her arms?

So what if Janelle was showing her how to bottle-feed the little furball?

So what if Stephie nuzzled her face into Bubba's soft, warm fur?

Hey, CHIMPS HAVE FUR TOO, you know!

(Am I shouting again? Sorry!)

Anyway, Stephie kept holding the little creature-thing as

Janelle collected hay from the nursery that we'd been keeping him in.

"Why are you doing that?" Stephie asked.

"It has Bubba's scent on it. We're going to spread it around the lion habitat so Golda, his momma, will remember his smell before we reintroduce them."

"Why did we separate them in the first place?" Stephie asked.

"He had some sort of parasite. We didn't want her to get it."

"But he's okay now, right?"

"Right."

The good news (from my perspective) was that Stephie only held Bubba another minute or so before she put him back in his stall and we headed out to the lion habitat.

Our first step was to coax Golda up a ramp and into a small holding pen. That way we could climb down into the habitat and spread out the hay . . . without becoming her afternoon kitty treat.

Well, that was *their* first step. *My* first step was to find a nice tree for some shade, stretch out, and examine the inside of my eyelids. (One of my specialties.)

Meanwhile, Janelle opened the gate and started calling, "Here Golda, come on big momma, c'mon girl."

But the lion did nothing until Stephie started

CLICK-ing . . . *CLOCK*-ing . . .

and

CLACK-ing

her tongue.

"What are you doing?" Janelle asked.

"That's what Lisa does to get her to come. I'm not good at it like she is, but sometimes . . . there," she pointed, "see?" As she spoke, Golda rose to her feet. Both girls watched as the big cat (all 375 pounds of her) lumbered up the ramp and into the pen. As she passed by, Stephie reached through the bars to touch her.

"Uh, I wouldn't do that," Janelle said.

"Why not?"

"Golda can get pretty cranky, and she looks a little hungry."

Stephie quickly pulled her hand back.

"Now, grab those," Janelle said, pointing to a big bucket and shovel, "and let's get to work."

Stephie did as she was told.

As they climbed down the ladder into the habitat where the cat normally stayed so visitors could see her, Stephie asked, "What am I supposed to do with these?"

"Start scooping up Golda's poop."

"Eeew!" Stephie gave a shiver.

"You wanted to help, didn't you?"

"Yeah, but—"

"Working with animals isn't always glamorous."

"You can say that again," a voice called from above.

They looked up to see Hector, who was carrying two large buckets of grain to the goat pens.

"So, how's *poop patrol*?" he asked.

Stephie made a face.

"Just pretend you're emptying a cat's litter box," he said. "For a *very* big cat."

Stephie noticed something on his face and asked, "What happened to your eye?"

"Nothing's wrong with my eye," he said.

"The left one looks all purple."

He shrugged. "One of the kids at school called me a Mexican."

"What's wrong with that?"

"I'm from Colombia."

"So he hit you?" Janelle said.

"Let's just say that me and his pals had a little discussion."

The girls traded looks. They knew all about Hector's "discussions."

"Looks painful," Janelle said.

Hector turned to continue his chores. "You should see the other guys."

Janelle called after him, "What are you going to tell Mom when she finds out? You know she'll see your eye."

Hector called back, "Not if I can find some makeup."

"Right." Janelle gave a nervous laugh.

It was a laugh Stephie wouldn't understand until later when she realized Hector wasn't the only one practicing deception.

A deception that just might cost Stephie her very life . . .

4

It's Spiderman!

"LADIES, PLEASE . . . LET GO OF ME!" Nick cried as he tossed and turned in his sleep, slapping at his arms. "No more autographs! Please, I'm just one man. Let go of me!"

Poor Nick. He was having a terrible time sleeping on the tiny cots Dr. Mooketsi had assigned them. And he was even less thrilled about the tiny shack that held the tiny cots.

Earlier, they'd dropped Kele off at her house. And although Lisa was grateful for the quiet to her ears, she was not grateful that Nick felt he had to take over.

"Where's the air conditioning?" he asked when they first entered the shack they would be sleeping in.

Dr. Mooketsi smiled. "Always making with the jokes, yes, Nick?" Setting the kerosene lantern on the table he continued, "Remember, we are out here in the bush, very far. For fresh air, you may leave the door open, but I would not suggest doing so now, during the evening."

"And why's that?" Dad asked.

"Because we have many curious animals and insects— some small, some large—that like to roam at night."

"How large?" Lisa asked nervously.

"Not to worry, Miss Lisa. If you do not bother them, they will not bother you."

"Does that include mosquitoes?" Nick asked, slapping at the third or fourth that had landed on his arm.

"That is why we have the mosquito netting," Dr. Mooketsi said. He pointed to the white, gauzy fabric hanging around each cot. "Tuck it around your mattress at night and they will not bother you."

Nick slapped at another mosquito. "Until then do you offer blood transfusions?"

Dr. Mooketsi chuckled. "You do not have mosquitoes in California?"

"Sure, but we don't raise them as pets."

"Nick . . ." Dad warned.

"Ah." Dr. Mooketsi smiled. "Another joke."

Glancing about the room, Nick asked, "And what about closet space?" (Nick really wasn't trying to be a pain. For him, it just came naturally.) "You know, some place to hang all my clothes?"

"There is the back of that chair," Dr. Mooketsi said, motioning to a single wooden chair under a small desk.

"Seriously?" Nick said. "I'm supposed to hang all my—"

Dad cut him off. "We'll be fine, Dr. Mooketsi. And thank you for your hospitality."

"Of course," the doctor said. Then, turning for the door, he added, "We will show you around the compound after a good night's rest. I am sure it has been a very long trip."

"And getting longer by the minute," Nick mumbled.

"Nick!"

Fortunately, Dr. Mooketsi didn't hear. But once the doctor left, Dad gave Nick his lecture on basic manners. One that Nick had heard more times than he could count but somehow kept forgetting.

Once he'd finished, they chose their cots, unpacked, and prepared for some much-needed rest.

Well, almost . . .

"What's that?" Nick pointed to a corner of the ceiling.

"What's what?" Lisa said.

"In the shadows, I saw something move."

Dad picked up the lantern, headed to the corner, and held up the light for a better look. "It seems to be some sort of spider."

"A spider!" Lisa cried. (Lisa loves spiders about as much as she loves airplane flights.)

"Looks more like a giant crab!" Nick teased. "The thing is huge!"

"Nick!"

"Where's my shoe?" he said. "I'm going to kill it."

"No, leave it!" Lisa cried.

"What?"

"We don't want to make it mad."

"How do dead spiders get mad?"

"Dr. Mooketsi said if we don't bother them, they won't bother us."

"Well, I'm already bothered." Nick found his shoe and raised it to throw.

"Nick," Dad warned. "I'm not so sure—"

Too late. Nick

FLUNG

his shoe at the spider or crab or whatever-it-was. (He would have swatted it, but the creature was so big Nick was afraid it might grab the shoe and swat *him*.)

The good news was that Nick missed. (Good news at least for the spider or crab or whatever-it-was.)

The bad news was it sent the giant critter scurrying off into the shadows.

"Nick!" Lisa cried.

"Relax," he said. "I took care of him."

"You don't see him?" she asked, trying her best to stay calm.

"Nah, we're good."

But Dad, knowing Lisa was still frightened, did his dad thing. "Hang on, sweetheart, I'll check." Still holding the lantern, he carefully searched the walls, then the ceiling, and finally dropped to his hands and knees to search under their cots.

"Looks like it's gone," he said, rising to his feet.

"See," Nick said. "I scared him off."

And for once he was right. He had scared it. Which is why it had darted down the wall, across the floor, and hid under Nick's cot—but not down on the floor where Dad had looked. To be extra safe, it had crawled up the cot's leg and clung to the underside of his mattress—completely hidden and secure. (Well, secure as far as the spider or crab or whatever-it-was was concerned.)

At last, the three Mulligans crawled into their cots and carefully tucked the mosquito netting around their mattresses so mosquitoes and other bugs could not get in. Unfortunately, that meant one creepy spider or crab or whatever-it-was could not get out. It was trapped inside Nick's netting . . . sharing his cot.

And now it was crawling across his arm. That's when Nick woke from his dream and saw that it was not some clinging fan begging for his autograph. Instead, it was

AAAAUGH!

the spider-crab thing.

Nick screamed, slapping and brushing at it as he leaped off his cot to get away. A pretty good plan except the cot was still surrounded by the netting . . . which meant Nick was still surrounded by the netting . . . which meant he got completely tangled in it and fell to the floor, screaming:

"Get it off! Get it off! Get it off!"

By the time Lisa and Dad came to the rescue, the poor guy had twisted and rolled around so much that he had wrapped himself from head to toe in the white gauze, making him look like a giant caterpillar inside a giant cocoon.

Speaking of giant caterpillars, the next morning wasn't much better for Nick when he and Lisa joined Dr. Mooketsi at the breakfast table and discovered that's exactly what he'd served them to eat.

"Caterpillars?" Nick asked.

"That is correct." Dr. Mooketsi smiled. "A rare treat for honored guests. Please, don't be shy. Eat as many as you wish."

5
Complications

THE NEXT MORNING, JANELLE WAS RUNNING laps in the gym with her P.E. class. Even though she was desperately sucking in air (something she was used to) and running in last place (again, something she was used to), it felt great being her real self again. Janelle had wanted to help Jessica, but she was glad it was over. Even more glad that nobody found out.

Well, not quite . . .

"Hey, Mulligan!" Coach Sally Buffton called her over to the side.

Gasping for breath, Janelle slowed to a stop and joined her.

"Great work yesterday," the coach said.

"Umm, thanks?" Janelle said, though she wasn't exactly sure what she (Jessica) had done.

"I mean doing all those pull-ups? A real inspiration to the class. And the way you climbed that rope." Coach Buffton shook her head. "Amazing. Didn't know you had it in you."

Janelle nodded. "Neither did I."

"And your limp," Coach said. "When you ran into the bleachers yesterday? It's totally gone."

"Limp?" Janelle asked.

"You said you didn't see them—something about wearing the wrong glasses."

"Oh, right," Janelle said, pretending to remember. With a nervous laugh, she asked, "Which leg was it again?"

"Your left."

"Yes, of course," Janelle said and took a couple of steps pretending to limp.

Coach Buffton frowned. "On second thought, I think it was your right."

"Yes, yes, my right," Janelle said and immediately switched limps to the other side.

Coach cocked her head quizzically.

Janelle pushed up her glasses and forced a giggle. "I guess I'm just *ambidextrous*." (Hey, she's Janelle Mulligan. She knows what that word means. Kind of.)

But the fun and games had only begun.

"Well, get back with the others," Coach said. "After warm-ups we're going to play a little basketball. Can't wait to see what the new *you* can do with that."

Janelle nodded and limped back into the race . . . when she heard

PSSSSST . . .

coming from behind the bleachers. She slowed down and saw Jessica motioning for her to join her.

She glanced back to the coach and when it was safe, crossed behind the bleachers to join her sister. But Jessica kept motioning for her to follow until they entered the girls' locker room.

"What's going on?" she asked.

"Change clothes with me," Jessica said.

"What?"

"Mrs. Crawly challenged the room across the hall to another spelling bee."

"*Another* spelling bee?"

"She says if we beat everybody in our grade, she'll give us a week off with no homework."

Janelle gave her a look.

Jessica shrugged. "What can I say, she's a spelling fanatic." She motioned to Janelle's shorts and T-shirt. "C'mon, switch with me," she said as she peeled off her sweater.

"But—"

"C'mon."

"Hey, Mulligan?" It was Coach Buffton. She'd entered from the gym. In just a moment she would be rounding the lockers and see them.

The girls were trapped . . . with no way out.

(Unfortunately . . . that wasn't exactly true.)

Spotting the bathroom stall, Jessica whispered, "Quick, in there."

Before Janelle could protest, Jessica grabbed her sister's hand and pulled her into the stall. They had barely made it inside and closed the door before Coach appeared around the lockers.

"You all right in there?" she called.

The girls froze.

"Mulligan?"

Jessica motioned for them to keep changing. The tight space caused a few misplaced elbows to hit a few faces, but they continued quickly and quietly.

Coach approached the stall. "You okay?"

They looked at each other in terror. Jessica nodded for Janelle to answer at the same time Janelle motioned for Jessica. When each guessed the other wouldn't, they both answered . . . just a second apart.

"Yes," Jessica said.

"Yes," Janelle said.

Coach Buffton frowned. "What's going on?"

Jessica paused then said, "Echo?" She motioned for Janelle to do the same.

Reluctantly, Janelle repeated, "Echo."

"Hmm," Coach said. "I didn't know the stall was that big. Well, get a move on. We're choosing sides."

"Okay," Jessica said.

"Okay," Janelle said.

After a few more elbows in a few more faces, they finished

changing—each girl wearing the other's clothes. As Jessica straightened her T-shirt, she motioned for Janelle to hide behind the door while she opened it.

Coach Buffton was still standing there, waiting.

"Sorry," Jessica said.

Coach shrugged. "When you gotta go, you gotta go."

"Right." Jessica started for the gym.

"Mulligan?"

She stopped.

"Your glasses?"

"Oh, right." Jessica dashed back to the stall and reached inside where Janelle handed them to her. *"Thanks,"* she silently mouthed.

"You're welcome," Janelle whispered back.

"What was that?" Coach asked.

"Nothing." Jessica pretended to cough as she turned back for the gym. "Nothing at all."

Coach Buffton stood a moment, frowning.

"Come on, Coach," Jessica called. "Let's pick those sides."

"Right," Coach said and turned to join her.

And Janelle remained hiding inside the stall . . . trying to remember how to catch her breath.

6

Dad to the Rescue

"SHE'S SO GOOD WITH HIM," DR. MOOKETSI whispered as he watched Lisa enter the baby elephant's stall.

Dad smiled. "Yes, Lisa has a way with animals. She's one of the reasons we started our wild animal park."

Dr. Mooketsi shook his head in wonder. Lisa had knelt beside the baby elephant who lay on his side in the hay.

"Hi, Thato," she softly said. "How's it going, fellow? Hey, boy . . ."

"Is he sleeping?" Dad whispered.

"No," Dr. Mooketsi said. "They sleep standing up. And then only three or four hours a day."

"You say he's not eaten or had water?"

"Since we rescued him, very little. Adult elephants eat

three hundred pounds of food a day. He's eaten only the tiniest fraction of that. Poor thing."

"And you're sure it's emotional?" Dad asked.

Dr. Mooketsi nodded. "He saw his mother killed, and when the family unit tried to protect her—they travel in families of six to twelve—the poachers killed them as well."

"All but Thato?"

"If Kele's father had not heard the gunshots and arrived to chase them off they would have killed Thato as well."

"Just for the ivory of their tusks." Dad shook his head. "Heartbreaking."

"And completely illegal."

"Okay, boy," Lisa quietly cooed. "I'm just going to lay down beside you, okay?"

"Lisa," Dad cautioned, "be careful."

She nodded as she slowly lay down behind him in the hay. "Thato won't hurt me, will you, boy?"

When he didn't move, she reached out a hand and rested it on his side. There was no reaction, just his chest rising and falling as he breathed. She scooted closer, pressing her face to the back of his neck.

"His skin looks really tough," Dad said. "Is that normal?"

Dr. Mooketsi nodded. "For most elephants, their skin can be over an inch thick. Compared to ours which is very thin—only about a twentieth of an inch."

Ever so gently, Lisa began scratching the back of Thato's neck.

"We try to keep him moist," Dr. Mooketsi said, "hosing

him down many, many times a day, but his dehydration is great. At two hundred pounds, a baby elephant his size should be drinking ten to fifteen gallons of water a day."

Lisa moved her hand behind Thato's ears and continued scratching. He seemed to like it.

Outside, she heard a pickup approaching. It made a strange whine, like metal rubbing against metal. A door slammed, the truck pulled away, and an all-too-familiar voice entered the barn. Not Nick's. He was still in bed. (Sleeping is his favorite hobby.)

"Hi, guys," Kele shouted.

The men turned and were about to quiet her, but they were too late.

Spotting Lisa she cried, "Oh, cool. You're with Thato. I wanted to get here earlier—my dad had to make some stops first. But—"

If she said anything else, no one heard. Her loud voice broke the gentle spell Lisa had created for Thato.

The baby elephant jerked and waved his trunk.

"Lisa, look out!" Dad cried.

Before Lisa could move, the big animal rolled to face her, kicking at her with his big feet.

Instantly, Dad was there.

"It's okay, Dad," Lisa said. "It's—"

But he would have none of it. "Get away!" he shouted at the animal, kicking at the elephant and scooping Lisa into his arms. One of his feet struck Thato's leg, causing it to cry out.

"Dad!"

"Mr. Mulligan!" Dr. Mooketsi shouted.

Thato rolled away from them, pulled into himself . . . and quietly whimpered.

"Dad!" Lisa squirmed, and he set her down.

He could only stare, as shocked at his outburst as they were. "I'm sorry," he said. "I really thought he was attacking. I thought . . . I'm sorry."

No one spoke as all eyes turned back to the elephant. The poor thing seemed worse than ever. Any trust and connection Lisa was forming between them had been shattered.

Maybe for good.

I want to make it clear Janelle was not blind as she raced down the hall to Mrs. Crawly's class. Well, at least not truly blind like Lisa. Still, without her glasses, she did make two mistakes.

MISTAKE #1: She accidentally snuck into Mr. Grumpton's math class instead of Mrs. Crawly's English class. (Hey, they were right next to each other.)

Not a major problem. The major problem came with:

MISTAKE #2: She found where Jessica's desk should have been and took her seat.

Again, no problem except for:

"Well, hello there." It was Chad Heartthumper, the cutest boy in the whole school (and some would say the universe).

By sitting at Chad Heartthumper's desk, she was now *sitting on Chad Heartthumper's lap!*

AUGH!

she screamed as she leaped to her feet.

Flipping his gorgeous bangs out of those gorgeous blue eyes, he asked, "Have we met?"

AUGH!

she cried, searching for the doorway.

Mr. Grumpton turned from the blackboard and asked, "Is there a problem?"

"Not for me," Chad said, giving his hair another flip.

"S-s-sorry," Janelle stammered as she stumbled toward what she hoped was the door . . . while crashing into a few desks along the way. "Wrong room, sorry!"

By the time she made it out the door, her face was redder than a stop sign with a bad sunburn. And it didn't get any better with Chad's parting words, "Stop by again—any time!"

It took a couple of minutes trying to catch her breath—not to mention to restart her heart—before Janelle finally entered Mrs. Crawly's room.

The spelling bee had just begun. Mrs. Crawly's all-star spellers stood on one side of the room; the super spellers from the other class stood at the opposite side.

"Long bathroom break," Mrs. Crawly said.

"Sorry," Janelle said as she lined up with the others.

"Uh, Jessica, our class is on that side of the room."

"Oh, sorry," Janelle said as she headed across the room, stumbling over another desk.

"Hey!" the student complained.

"Sorry!"

And then another, "Watch it!"

"Sorry," she said again. "Sorry!"

By the time she found her place in the line, it was her turn.

"So, Jessica," Mrs. Crawly said, "spell *fraudulence*."

Janelle took a breath and began. "Fraudulence. F-r-a-u-d-u-l-e-n-c-e."

You could practically hear Mrs. Crawly sigh in relief. Not only was winning important to her life, it *was* her life.

As the contest continued, each word grew harder and harder. Kids from both sides were dropping out and taking their seats. Soon it was her turn again.

"Jessica, your word is *untrustworthy*."

"Untrustworthy," Jessica said. "U-n-t-r-u-s-t-w-o-r-t-h-y."

"Yes!" Mrs. Crawly whispered under her breath.

It may have felt like a victory for Mrs. Crawly, but for Janelle, the guilt grew heavier and heavier. Why did each word given to her seem to point out her dishonesty? Okay, fine. The next word she would misspell on purpose and sit down.

Unfortunately, the next round was even harder. Nearly

everyone missed and had to take their seat—everyone but Janelle from Mrs. Crawly's room and the geeky Brian Brainbruiser from the other class.

"Brian," Mrs. Crawly said, "your word is *fabricator*."

Brian pushed up his glasses and swallowed so hard Janelle could hear his Adam's apple bob.

"Brian?" Mrs. Crawly repeated.

He cleared his throat. "Fabricator." He began to spell, his voice squeaking like a rusty hinge. "Fabricator. F-a-b-r-i-c-a-t-e-r. Fabricator."

A hush fell over the room.

Finally, Mrs. Crawly answered, "That is incorrect. I'm so sorry, Brian." (She might have sounded more convincing if she hadn't giggled as he took his seat.)

She turned to Janelle. If Janelle got this right, the room would be one step closer to being champions.

"Jessica, can you spell *fabricator*?"

Now was the time. Time to come clean. Time to be honest. Time to take a stand . . . or, in her case, a seat.

"Jessica?"

But Mrs. Crawly sounded so hopeful. This was all the poor woman lived for. (Well, that, and rocky road ice cream with caramel sauce.) And what about Jessica's class? Everyone was depending on her.

"C'mon, Mulligan," Chloe whispered from her desk. That's right, even Chloe—who had not only misspelled *humble*, but had no idea what it meant—was rooting her on. It was a big deal to beat the other class in something.

If Janelle spelled *fabricator* correctly, everyone would win: Jessica. Mrs. Crawly. The entire class.

"Jessica?" Mrs. Crawly repeated.

She took a deep breath. Then another. (If she took any more, her lungs would explode.) Finally, she answered, "Fabricator. F-a-b-r-i-c-a-t-o-r. Fabricator."

The room again filled with silence. Everyone waited. Until . . .

"That's right!" Mrs. Crawly cried. "I won, er, *we* won. I mean, the class won!"

Janelle couldn't tell for sure, but without her glasses, it looked as if Mrs. Crawly was doing some sort of victory dance. In fact, the entire class was clapping, cheering, and *Oh, yeah!*-ing.

Well, the entire class minus one. Janelle Mulligan suspected she hadn't won at all, but had instead lost something important.

7

Road Trip

"HI, MIKE, YOU'RE ON SPEAKERPHONE," Mom spoke into her phone set on the dinner table.

"Hi, guys," Dad said back.

Everyone shouted, "How's it going, Dad?" "Hi, Dad." "Miss you, Dad." "When you coming home, Dad?"

Which, at Dad's end sounded like: "Hi, Dad." "How's it going, Dad?" "Miss you, Dad." "When are you coming home, Dad?"

Along with a little

OO-oo AH-ah EE-ee

thrown in by yours truly.

Mealtime at the Mulligans is one of my favorite times.

Actually, mealtime *any*time is one of my favorite times. Normally, I'm not allowed to join in . . . unless Stephie disguises me in one of her costumes. Or I hide under the table or on top of the refrigerator. I tried hiding inside once, but that was a chilling experience. (Get it? Chilling experience? The other animals thought it was funny . . . at least the laughing hyenas did.)

Anywho . . .

We were all gathered around the table eating something Julie helped Mom fix—a jiggly, green-looking something Julie proudly said was yummy mashed potatoes—and which Mom promised wasn't poisonous. (Probably true. How can something be poisonous when you can't swallow it?)

"So how are things?" Mom asked Dad over the phone.

"Everything's great," Dad said. "Africa's great, Lisa's great—"

"I'm great," Nick called from the background. "No, strike that—what's *greater* than great?"

Everyone groaned—something almost required by law when Nick is boasting about something.

As they talked, I made my move. I casually pulled Stephie's plate of jiggly-green thingy over to my place. It didn't exactly look "yummy," but food is food, right?

"How are you?" Mom asked Dad. "And how's that baby elephant?"

"I'm afraid I messed up," Dad said. "Lisa was making progress with him, but then I thought he was attacking her and . . . well, I was a jerk and ruined things."

"He wasn't a jerk," Lisa said. "He was just being, you know, a dad."

"A little overprotective of his daughter?" Mom asked.

"Always," Lisa sighed. Then, changing the subject, she asked, "So how are things with Golda and Bubba?"

Stephie spoke up. "I tried that clicking thing you do with your tongue. I did pretty good, but nobody trusts me."

"Sweetheart . . ." Mom disagreed.

"But I'll be even better with practice."

"That's great," Lisa said.

Janelle added, "We're going to reintroduce Bubba to Golda tomorrow."

"Well, be careful," Lisa said. "You know how 'over-protective' parents can be."

"Hey!" Dad said, pretending to be offended.

"Hi, Daddy," little Julie called from the end of the table. "I helped Mommy fix dinner."

"That's super, kiddo. I bet it's definitely yummy."

Everyone got quiet, not wanting to hurt the little munchkin's feelings.

Jessica finally answered. "Well, it's definitely original."

"That's right!" we all agreed.

"It really is." "It really is something." "Yum-yum."
"It sure is." "You said it." "Great stuff."
"Oo-oo AA-aa EE-ee."

"And Hector," Dad asked, "how are you doing?"

"He's at the reptile house, feeding the snakes," Janelle said.

"This time of night?"

"He's been really helpful," Mom said. "So much so that I barely see him."

Stephie and Janelle traded looks. Mom didn't know it, but that's exactly what Hector wanted . . . to not be seen. At least until his black eye healed.

I'd like to tell you about the rest of the phone call, but I had finally worked up the courage to bite into Julie's jiggly-green thingy. And, no matter what the others said, it really wasn't that bad, especially after I hopped off my chair, raced outside, and spit it out. It was even better after I turned on the hose and rinsed my mouth a couple of times.

Later that morning, in Botswana, Lisa and the group finished packing the open-air van. "So have we got everything?" Dad asked.

"Actually, a bit more than everything." Dr. Mooketsi chuckled as he loaded Nick's third suitcase. "Are you sure you do not wish to bring the big screen TV?"

"Do we have one?" Nick asked.

Dr. Mooketsi laughed. "Always making with the jokes."

"I still don't get why we're going on this overnight thing," Nick said. "Wasn't last night uncomfortable enough?"

Dr. Mooketsi sat behind the wheel as the others climbed in. "You cannot enjoy the great wildlife of my country from inside a hut."

"I don't know about that," Lisa teased. "Nick had quite a bit of it crawling on his arm last night."

Dr. Mooketsi grinned, dropped the van into gear, and they began

Bang-ing . . . **Buck**-ing . . .

and

Bounce . . . BOUNCE . . . BOUNCE-ing

down the dirt road. (It wasn't as bad as the airplane flight, but Nick was still glad he packed a couple of extra air sickness bags.)

As he drove, Dr. Mooketsi explained, "I am afraid we gave little Thato quite the scare."

"Sorry about that," Dad said.

"Not to worry. But let us give him some time to settle. In the meantime, I thought you would like to see some of the elephants we hope will adopt him into their family."

"How do we know the poachers won't get them?" Nick asked.

Dr. Mooketsi let out a long sigh. "We don't. They are becoming bolder every day. So we can only hope."

"And pray," Lisa said.

"Yes, Miss Lisa. And pray."

Five minutes later, they pulled up to Kele's house, just as her dad was leaving. His pickup made the same whining sound of metal scraping against metal that Lisa had heard before.

Once Kele joined them and hopped in, she couldn't wait to start talking. And once she started, everyone couldn't wait for her to stop.

"So, Lisa, what do you think about helping Thato?"

"Well, did you—"

"I think you did great."

"Well, I—"

"And everyone says you've got a great way with animals."

"Thanks, but I—"

It was just like the other ride with Kele. And as soon as she got tired of *not* listening to Lisa's answers about Thato, she began *not* listening about their trip.

"Have you ever been on a safari before?"

"No, I—"

"It's not a *real* safari because we're just spending a night."

"Right, and I—"

"We're camping near the river."

"That's what I—"

"I love camping. Do you camp much at home? I don't get to do it as much as . . ."

It wasn't exactly the same as when we all talked at once to Dad on the phone, but her words came so fast that they soon all blurred together.

"*. . . but I'm really excited to come with you and show you all around the cool stuff especially the ones you probably don't have back home...*"

And just when they were all a little worried that she'd forget to breathe, they heard:

" . . . but I think my absolute favorite thing is . . . oh, look, a crocodile!"

"Crocodile?" Nick cried.

"Yes, right there." She pointed to the side of the road. "He's sunning himself. Dr. Mooketsi, pull over, pull over!"

"Yes, of course." The doctor brought them to a stop beside the giant reptile.

Nick looked over his side of the open van. It was three feet away. "Um . . ."

"Not to worry," Dr. Mooketsi said. "Keep your door shut and you will be fine."

Not entirely convinced, Nick tried another argument. "Um . . ."

"Have you never seen one?" Kele asked. "This close?"

"Of course I have." Nick coughed nervously. "But mostly as handbags and cowboy boots."

"You mean the skin?" Kele cried in horror.

"Right. Without all the bothersome claws and teeth."

"What a terrible thing to say! They are very majestic creatures. Here, let me show you." She threw open her door and hopped out on her side.

"Kele," Dr. Mooketsi warned.

"I'll only be a minute."

"Be careful."

"Of course."

She grabbed a long, thick branch from the side of the road and crossed over to Nick's side. She stretched it out and gently nudged the big creature's belly. It gave a loud

hisssssss . . .

"Kele." Dr. Mooketsi sounded more concerned.

"I'll be careful." She poked it a little harder. "I want to show Nick how powerful they can be and why—"

The crocodile opened its huge jaws and lunged at the branch. Before Kele could pull it back, the giant creature snapped it in two.

"Kele!" Dr. Mooketsi shouted.

She didn't need a second invitation. Dropping the branch, she raced to her side of the van, hopped in, and slammed the door.

She turned to Nick out of breath. "See how powerful and majestic they are?"

Nick looked down at the animal, just feet below him as it continued thrashing and attacking the branch.

"Uh, Dr. Mooketsi?" Nick's voice trembled.

Dr. Mooketsi gave his trademark chuckle as he dropped the van into gear.

Lisa teased, "You sound scared, Nick."

"Me?" Nick's voice cracked. "Nah. Like the doctor says, they can't crawl up into vans."

"Yes," Dr. Mooketsi said. "That is usually the case."

"Usually?"

8

Night Visitors

IT WAS 2:34 IN THE MORNING. Janelle stared at the wall unable to sleep. It wasn't happening, especially with Jessica

snoOOOOOORR-ing

like a chain saw in the bunk above her.

All day long, guilt had been piling up in Janelle's head and upon her heart. Earlier, she had decided to go to bed before Jessica and snuggle up to her Bible. Reading God's Word always made Janelle feel better.

Well, almost always. It wasn't as effective on a day when she was dishonest about spelling bees . . . and then lying to cover up that lying . . . and lying to, well, you get the idea.

It also didn't help when the verse she first opened her Bible to, from Proverbs, seemed to leap off the page at her: *"The LORD detests lying lips, but he delights in people who are trustworthy."*

Okay, fine. But that was just one verse. She flipped over to Psalms, one of her favorite books in the Bible, only to read: *"All who swear by God will glory in him, while the mouths of liars will be silenced."*

Yikes! It was almost like God was talking to her.

That's why when Jessica finally came into the room to get ready for bed, Janelle broke the news to her . . .

"I can't . . ." she said. "I . . . I don't want to do this anymore."

Janelle was more than a little surprised when Jessica said, "Okay."

"Okay?"

"Sure. Of course, you and I will be doing after-school detention for the rest of our lives." (Do they have detention in college?) "Oh, and I just told Mom how great I'm doing in the spelling bee. She couldn't be prouder of us."

"Of *you*," Janelle said.

"Of *us*," Jessica said. "She knows I couldn't do it on my own, so I told her you've been helping me study the words."

"Jessica! That's another lie."

"Maybe it is, maybe it isn't."

"Maybe it . . . What does that mean?"

"Tomorrow's the final spelling bee, the championship for our entire grade."

"Meaning?"

"If you're so worried, you've got all tonight to teach me."

"Jessica!"

"I'm just saying." Jessica reached for the dictionary on their desk and tossed it at her. "Here."

Janelle stared at the giant book. "I can't teach you every word in here!"

"Totally your call," Jessica said as she climbed up to her bunk. "We get busted for lying . . . or you teach me what's in there."

Janelle looked back at the Bible in one hand . . . then to the dictionary in the other. It would be difficult . . . maybe impossible. But if staying up all night was what it took . . . well, all right.

With a deep breath, she opened the dictionary to the first page. She found the first word and read it out loud. "Aardvark." She waited. "Jess, do you know how to spell *aardvark*?"

Still no answer.

"Jess? Jessica—"

snoOOOOORR . . .

"Jessica?"

No answer. Just her sister

snoOOORR-ing

from the top bunk.

It was hopeless. Totally hopeless. She closed the dictionary and looked back down at her Bible. She opened it again, flipping back to Proverbs. And there, in front of her, were the words: *"A faithful witness does not lie, but a false witness breathes out lies."*

She closed her eyes. One more day. One more day and it would all be over. If they didn't get caught, everything would work out. At least that's what she told herself.

Though, somehow, she suspected that just might be another lie . . .

SHREEEEEEEK—ahhh . . .

Nick froze. "What's that sound?"

Kele laughed. "Just a fish eagle."

"Being tortured to death?"

Kele giggled. "It's probably fishing near the water. It's nothing to be scared of."

"Who said I'm scared?" (He'd be more convincing if the fork in his hand stopped shaking long enough to get some food on it.) "There's nothing to be scared about."

The group had arrived at the campsite and had finished setting up their tents for the night. Now they were gathered around the campfire for dinner.

"The night is full of many sounds," Dr. Mooketsi said.

"It's not the sounds I'm worried about," Nick said as he reached for the mosquito spray to give himself a third coat. "It's the—"

RUMBLE . . . GROWL . . . LAUGH

Once again, he froze.

"Cool," Kele said. "Sounds like some hippos are nearby."

"Hippos?" Lisa asked. She was definitely excited. "Is that what they sound like? Sounded a little like laughing."

"Yeah," Kele said. "Pretty cool, huh?"

"But their voices." Lisa leaned forward to better hear. "They're so deep and low."

"*Infrasound*," Dr. Mooketsi said. "Much of it is below what we humans can hear."

RUMBLE . . . GROWLLL . . . GROAAAANNN . . .

Nick tried not to shiver. "I hear that just fine."

"Hippos," Lisa repeated in awe. "I wish they were closer."

"They are quite shy," Dr. Mooketsi said. "They mostly come out of the water at night. And they can be very dangerous."

"Will we see any?" Dad asked.

"If we were closer to the river, perhaps. But we are too far away now."

"I can take them," Kele said. "I know the area."

Before she could answer, Dad did his dad thing. "Thanks, Kele, that's very thoughtful, but let's save that for tomorrow."

"But Dad," Lisa argued. "Dr. Mooketsi just said they only come out at night."

"I appreciate that, but it's dark—"

"Guys?" Nick said.

"—and who knows what you might run across."

"Guys!"

"But Kele says she knows the way and—"

"GUYS!" Nick shouted.

They all turned to him as he pointed a shaky finger into the dark. "How come those bushes are moving?"

"Which ones?" Dad asked.

"All of them!"

Suddenly the bushes exploded with—

"Monkeys!" Nick cried. "GIANT MONKEYS!"

"Not monkeys!" Kele shouted. "Baboons!"

There was a dozen of them, about three feet tall with long arms. And they seemed to be coming from every direction.

"Quick!" Dr. Mooketsi yelled. "Grab the food! Get it into the van!"

Nick shouted, "How about getting *us* into the van?"

"They've come only to raid," Dr. Mooketsi said as he scooped up his bowl of stew and grabbed the loaf of bread. "It's doubtful they'll hurt us."

"Doubtful?" Nick cried—just as one of the critters leaped in front of him. It stretched out its hand for his plate.

"This is mine!" Nick shouted.

The animal grabbed it and pulled.

Nick pulled it back.

The animal pulled harder.

Nick pulled harder.

The animal

Shreeeek-ed

and bared some rather large (and not to mention razor-sharp) fangs.

"Right." Nick let go. "I see your point."

But Kele wasn't giving up so easily. As another baboon raced at her, she scrambled up onto a rock. Raising her hands high over her head she let out a mighty

ROAR!

The animal came to a stop. Whatever crazy this human girl had, he didn't appear to want it.

She leaped from the rock with her hands still over her head. She began waving them back and forth as she charged toward the baboon. The poor thing was so startled that it turned and ran for its life . . . but not before scooping up Lisa's nearby windbreaker.

"Hey!" Dad yelled.

"Let him keep it," Dr. Mooketsi shouted. "Let's just get the food into the van!"

But they were outnumbered. Within minutes the baboons had found every scrap of food that did not make it into the van. Even the utensils, along with the pepper shaker whose lid one curious creature managed to unscrew and stick his nose into.

ACHOO!

As the group waited in the van, the baboons scoured the camp, taking everything in sight, including Nick's last can of mosquito spray.

"Hey, I need that!" he shouted.

To which the baboon replied:

SHREEEK!

"Right, right," Nick said. "Please, help yourself."

The baboons disappeared as suddenly as they had appeared. They raced back into the bush with their prizes, never to be seen or heard from again . . . except for the distant and fading:

ACHOO . . .

Achoo . . .

Achoo . . .

9

Major Misadventure

SINCE BOTSWANA IS NINE HOURS AHEAD OF US, it was nighttime for Dad but only morning for us when he called again. So there we were, in the car heading to school, having another speakerphone call with him. He sounded kind of homesick. But that's okay. We really missed him too.

Anyhow, remember when I said I wasn't jealous about Stephie and Bubba? Well, I was even less jealous than when I wasn't jealous back then—when I said I wasn't jealous. (I think I just sprained my brain.) So it was a total and complete accident when, here in the car, I sort of threw myself onto Stephie's lap and rolled onto my back begging and

Whimper . . . whimper . . . whimper-ing

for a good belly rub.

"What's wrong, Winona?" she asked. "You okay?"

Sure, I was okay. And even if I wasn't, my mood had absolutely *nothing* to do with any jealousy about my friend being on the phone telling Dad how excited she was about returning the goofy-looking furball cub to his mother.

"That's terrific, kiddo," Dad said. "But be careful. Lions can be unpredictable, especially when it comes to their cubs."

"Don't worry," Stephie said. "I'll have Janelle with me the whole time."

What about me? I thought. But what came out sounded a lot like:

whimper . . . whimper . . . whimper

with a little

whine

thrown in to make my point.

If Dad heard, he didn't let on. "That's great, Steph," he said. "Staying close to Janelle is important."

"Yes," Stephie said, "but it's not like I need her."

"Of course not," Dad said. "But we have to make her feel useful, right?"

"Right."

He gave a quiet chuckle and then asked Mom, "You said you had some good news?"

"I'll say. Jessica is on her way to becoming the star speller of her seventh-grade class."

"Wow, that's terrific," Dad said. "Who would have thought?"

"Not me," Janelle mumbled.

Jessica quickly jumped in. "But Janelle helped. Without her, there's no way I could ever have done this."

"You can say that again," Janelle said, then threw in an extra "Ow!" when her twin's elbow landed in her ribs.

Mom continued, "After school today they're having a spelling bee competition for everyone in her grade."

"Great," Dad said. "Are you going?"

"NOOO!" the twins shouted in unison.

Mom threw a concerned look at them in her rearview mirror.

Jessica quickly explained, "I . . . I mean with all the work you've got to do at the park."

"All that veterinarian stuff," Janelle said.

"And all the bossing everyone around," Jessica added.

"And—"

"All right, all right," Mom said, laughing. "I get it. You don't want me around to embarrass you."

The girls relaxed, but only until Mom said, "Still, it would be fun."

"Mom," Jessica argued. "It's just the seventh-grade class, not the whole school. Even Janelle's eighth-graders won't be there." (You do remember Jessica saying that Janelle skipped a grade because she is so smart, right?)

"Just the same," Dad said, "if your mother can support Jess, I think that would be terrific."

If the twins were worried before, they were downright terrified now.

Mom sighed. "But . . . I'm afraid the girls are right. I have so much on my plate."

The twins let out a sigh of relief.

"But we'll see."

The twins sucked in a gasp of fear.

"So tell me," Mom said, "how's it going with Nick and Lisa?"

"For the most part, they're real troupers."

"Even Nick?"

"I said, 'for the most part.'"

Mom chuckled.

"Right now, everyone's tucked into their tents and getting some sleep. I've got to say, I'm really proud of them."

"Me too," Mom said. She smiled at the twins in the mirror. "Isn't it great to see children growing up, on their way to being responsible adults?"

"Absolutely."

Both girls looked down at the floor, feeling anything but responsible.

"Well, I'd better sign off," Dad said. "Got a big day ahead of us here. A big day for you guys too."

"Love you, Michael," Mom said.

"Love you too," he said. "And girls, I've just got to say again how proud I am of you . . . how proud I am of the whole family."

Stephie beamed.

And the twins? Well, if they stared any harder at the floor, they would have bored holes through it.

Dad might not have been quite so proud of his kids if he knew what they were really up to. Especially Lisa . . .

"Are you sure this is safe?" she whispered as they headed down the path.

"Absolutely," Kele said. "I've been this way to the river like a million times. And Dr. Mooketsi didn't say *no*."

"Right, but my dad—"

"Didn't say no, either. Not officially."

"Right, but—"

"And you want to get closer to those hippos, right?"

"Yes, but aren't they danger—"

"We won't get *that* close. And it'll only take an hour or so. We'll be back before anyone knows we're gone."

Lisa gave a reluctant sigh.

"Oh, and Lisa?"

"Yeah?"

"You might want to take my hand."

"Thanks," Lisa said, "but unless there's a problem, I'm perfectly capable of walking on my own."

"Would a problem be like that giant Cape cobra right in front of us?"

"A giant Cape—"

"Shhh . . ." Kele grabbed Lisa's hand and yanked her to the side of the path. Without a word—but with lots of nervous breathing on Lisa's part—the two girls carefully moved around the snake.

Once they were out of harm's way and back on the path Lisa asked, "Are Cape cobras dangerous?"

"Only if you don't like dying."

"Okay." Lisa took another breath. "Thanks."

"No problem," Kele said. "So how long have you been blind? You don't mind me asking, do you?"

"No, of course not," Lisa answered. "All of my life."

"Wow. And you don't like people . . . helping you?"

"Not unless I ask or if—" She was suddenly stopped by a

Squish, squish, squish-ing

under her feet. "What's that?" Lisa asked.

"No worries. You're wearing shoes."

"Right, but what—"

"We have really big cockroaches around here. They like traveling at night."

"Eeew!"

"Don't worry, they're not dangerous. A little gooey, but like I said, you're wearing shoes. Of course, if you were barefoot . . ."

"Right." Lisa gave a shudder. "I get the picture."

"So," Kele said, "you don't like people helping you?"

"Not unless I ask for help, or if there's some obstacle I can't see."

"Like deadly cobras?"

"Or giant cockroaches."

Kele nodded. "Got it."

They continued down the moonlit path. As they drew closer to the river, they heard the hippos' rumblings, growling, and weird laughter suddenly stop.

"What happened?" Lisa asked.

"I'm not sure," Kele said. "Hippos have a great sense of smell. Maybe they caught scent of all that mosquito spray you and your brother used. Or maybe—" She was interrupted by a loud

POP!

"What's that?" Lisa asked.

"I don't know," Kele said. "Unless it's

POP! POP!

gunfire."

"Gunfire?" Lisa said. "At night? Who would be shooting guns in the middle of the—"

POP! POP! POP!

And then they heard something else . . . a sound Lisa would never forget. It was a

half scream . . .

half cry . . .

(And definitely NOT human)

"Kele, what's that—"

"Elephants!" Kele whispered.

"Elephants?"

"Someone's shooting them!"

"Who would be shooting elephants in the middle of the—"

"Poachers! Quick!" Kele grabbed her hand. "C'mon!"

They started running. Lisa had just one more question:

"If that's gunfire and they're shooting at elephants . . . why are we running *toward* it?"

"To stop them!"

10
Major Misadventure Times Two

SCHOOL FINALLY ENDED, and the great spelling bee (better known as the *great lie*) was about to begin.

Mrs. Crawly frittered and fretted about the auditorium, afraid no one would show. (What did she expect? It was just a spelling bee for seventh-graders.)

Meanwhile, the twins stood backstage making last-minute preparations.

"Okay," Jessica said. "It's just you against the top speller from each of the other classes. You can do this."

"You mean *you* can do it," Janelle said.

"That's what I said. Easy peezy, no sweat."

"Except for my hands." They looked at Janelle's hands.

Not only were they shaking, but her palms were wetter than a swimming pool in a flooded river in the middle of the ocean.

"Just nerves," Jessica said. "I promise you, this will be the very last time."

Janelle took a deep breath.

"And remember to limp," Jessica said.

"Because . . ."

"You hurt your leg in gym class, remember?" She reached for Janelle's glasses. "Because you were wearing these stupid glasses." She pulled them from Janelle's face and added, "Which you won't be wearing now because—"

Another voice answered, "Because she's you."

The girls spun around to see Chloe stepping from behind the curtains.

"How long have you been there?" Jessica demanded.

"Long enough," Chloe said. "I knew Jessica was too dim for any of this to be real."

"What are you talking about?" Jessica said as she slipped on Janelle's glasses. "I'm Janelle."

"And look at my leg," Janelle said, taking a step and pretending to limp.

"Uh, it's the other one, sis."

"Exactly," Janelle said, switching legs.

Chloe snickered. "What type of fool do you think I am?"

"How many types are there?" Jessica asked.

Janelle whispered, "I don't think that's helping."

"So what are you going to do?" Jessica demanded. "Rat on us?"

"Hmm," Chloe said. She would have frowned, but that would put a wrinkle in the perfect skin of her perfect forehead. "If I do that, our class will lose. Of course, you would be totally in the wrong, but Mrs. Crawly might also blame me."

"Ah," Janelle said, pretending to see her point.

Chloe continued. "And if I don't tell on you, our class will probably win, *and* you'll both owe me big time!"

"Owe you by doing what?" Janelle said.

"By joining my devoted fans, silly."

"Meaning . . ."

"Oh, you know. Opening doors so I don't dirty my hands, fetching lunch so I don't stand in line with common people, and of course, answering all my fan mail."

"You have fan mail?" Janelle asked.

"Not yet, but soon. With this face, this hair, these clothes . . . how could I not?"

"Listen," Jessica said, "I don't know who you think you are, but there's no way—"

"Oh hi, Mom!" Janelle cried.

Jessica spun around to see Mom join them.

"What are you doing here?" Janelle asked.

"I've come to take you home," she said.

"Home?"

"To help Stephie with Bubba."

Before either girl could answer, Chloe spoke up. "Well, hello, Mrs. Mulligan. Aren't you looking lovely today?"

"Well thank you, Chloe."

"And might I say those jeans you've selected are a tasteful match with that lovely sweatshirt."

If Janelle rolled her eyes any harder, they'd just keep spinning around in her head.

"Oh, these?" Mom said. "I've just come from work."

"Seriously?" Chloe said. "Who would have known. You look as fresh as a spring day."

"I think I'm going to get sick," Jessica muttered.

"Not as sick as if she busts us," Janelle whispered back.

"Oh, Jessica," Mom said. "I just talked to Mrs. Crawly. She's willing to wait a few minutes so I can rush Janelle home and get back here to watch you."

"Watch me!" both twins cried in unison.

Then, trading looks, Jessica said, "You mean, watch *me*?"

"Well, who else would I watch?"

"Right," Jessica said, trying to hide the panic in her voice. "I was kind of hoping Janelle could stick around. You know, to enjoy all the work she's put in—tutoring me and everything. Right, sis?"

Janelle coughed nervously. "Right."

Mom smiled. "That's so sweet. But remember, this is also Stephie's big day. She's in the car waiting, and she's really been looking forward to reuniting Golda with her cub."

It was Jessica's turn to cough. "So you're taking Janelle home and coming back to watch *me*."

"Of course. You're my daughter too. And I couldn't be prouder."

"But . . . I really need Janelle here," Jessica said.

Janelle added, "To practice that last set of words."

"And for moral support!" Jessica added.

"That's right!" Janelle said.

Mom hesitated . . .

Chloe came to the rescue. "You've got nothing to worry about, Mrs. Mulligan." She turned and gave the girls her best smile (better known as her best sneer). "I'll be here to give Jessica all the help she needs."

"You'd do that for her?" Mom asked.

"Of course," Chloe said, then gave them another "smile." "What are friends for?"

"How sweet," Mom said. "Well, let's get a move on, Janelle. I need to hurry back to cheer on your sister!"

11
Things Get Worse

LISA AND KELE RAN INTO THE NIGHT.

"This is crazy!" Lisa shouted.

"Not if we can save them!" Kele yelled back. "Keep hanging on to my hand!"

Normally, Lisa wasn't fond of being led around. But since she was in the middle of Africa, running through thick brush and tall grass, she made this one exception.

Eventually, the shots stopped.

But there were those other sounds. The

SCREAMING

and

CRYING

of the elephants.

Oh, and one other sound. The elephants' legs

SWOOSHING

through the grass. Along with the

THUD, THUD, THUD-ing

of some very heavy feet racing toward them.

"Kele?" Lisa cried.

"It's the herd!" Kele shouted.

"Why are . . . are they attacking us?"

"They're not attacking."

"Are you sure? Because"—

THUD, THUD, THUD

—"it sure sounds like it!"

"They can't see us! They have terrible eyesight."

"But—"

"It'll be okay . . . unless they trample us by accident."

"Trample us by acci—"

SWOOSH THUD

SWOOSH THUD

SWOOSH THUD

"Over here!" Kele dragged her behind a large tree . . . just as the herd—eight giant elephants—thundered past so close that Lisa could have reached out and touched them. She wasn't sure how long they were huddled behind the tree like that before the herd finally passed.

"You okay?" Kele asked.

When she finally found her voice Lisa squeaked, "Sure."

Kele jumped to her feet and again grabbed her hand. "C'mon!" She started to run.

"Where are we going?" Lisa demanded.

"We've got to catch them!"

"The elephants?"

"The poachers!"

"I don't think that's such a good—"

"Oh no . . ." Kele slowed to a stop.

"Now what?"

"Can't you see?"

"Uh, not one of my specialties."

"We're too late." Kele dropped to her knees, then began to quietly sniff.

"Kele?"

When she answered, her voice was clogged with emotion. "They killed her."

Lisa knelt down. She reached out and felt an animal with thick, rough skin . . . exactly like baby Thato's at the compound.

Kele began crying. "They took her tusks. Just now. They killed her and took them."

Lisa had no words.

"And her tail," Kele sobbed.

"Her tail?"

"They take them for luck."

Lisa laid her hand on Kele's arm and quietly said, "I'm so sorry."

Kele nodded and continued to cry. Only then did Lisa hear something else. "Listen," she said. "Do you hear that?"

Kele shook her head.

"No," Lisa repeated, "listen."

Kele strained to hear. Over the chirping crickets and strange night sounds came the distant voices of . . . men.

"They're still here," Kele whispered.

"The poachers?"

"Yeah."

Along with the voices came the faint sound of laughter.

Slowly, without a word, Kele rose to her feet.

Lisa joined her.

Kele reached out and took her hand. "C'mon."

"Where are we going?"

"Someone has to stop them."

"Kele!"

"C'mon!"

12

And Worser . . .

I DID MY USUAL JUMPING UP AND DOWN—ONE FOOT,
then the other—as Mom pulled into the driveway with
Stephie and Janelle. Like I said, me and Stephie are close.
The fact that she always saves food from her meals and slips
it to me later doesn't hurt. (Particularly if it's dessert.)

But today was different.

Not different for me. I was my usual cool and stylin' self.
I'd already cleaned up by licking my arms—over and under
(yum)—and picking between my toes (double yum). Now
that I was perfectly groomed, I waited, totally calm . . . until
Stephie opened the car door. That's when I threw myself into
her arms, quietly screaming, at the top of my lungs:

OO-oo AH-ah EE-ee!

(Chimps can get a little emotional.)

And for good reason. It had been six whole hours without my best friend (and her snacks).

"Oh, hi, girl," she said as she pulled my hands from around her neck and set me on the ground.

That's it? That's all I was getting?

I jumped into her arms again . . . screaming another hello while searching her pockets for treats.

"Okay, girl, that's enough."

Enough? There's never enough when it comes to chimp love . . . or chimp hunger. I cocked my head and asked for an explanation.

OO-oo Ah . . .

But she cut me off and turned to Janelle. "This is going to be great," she said.

Going to be great? I thought. This is already great. I'm here. She's here. How could it get better? (Well, except for that treat . . .)

But I soon discovered she was talking about somebody other than me. Hard to imagine, I know.

"You kids be careful," Mom called from the front seat of the car. "Make sure you're completely out of the habitat before opening the pen for Golda."

"Right," Janelle said.

"I know you've been practicing, but this is important."

"Right," Janelle said.

"No short cuts."

"Right."

"And remember . . ."

I'm guessing Janelle wasn't paying much attention to what came after that. (And I won't put you to sleep by telling you.) Let's just say Mom quoted all the stuff they teach in Mom School. And since she got straight A's in "How to Worry about Everything," it took a few minutes. When she'd covered what to do if the earth was struck by a giant asteroid, she turned the car around and headed back to school . . . but not before reminding us one last time to "be careful!"

"We will," Stephie called.

"Right," Janelle mumbled.

Stephie took Janelle's hand, and after some brief

whimper-ing

from me, she also took mine. "Let's go," she said as we headed for the lion cub's nursery. "This will be fun."

But the look on Janelle's face said she was having anything but fun. We didn't learn until later that it was because of what was about to happen back at the spelling bee. Her sister was about to make a total fool of herself . . . *if* the twins were lucky.

If they were *un*lucky they'd both be busted for lying.

As we passed the lion habitat, Stephie called out to

Golda. "Hello, momma. We're going to get your baby right now."

Janelle's mind was definitely someplace else. And you didn't have to be a genius (let alone a chimp) to know it was still with her twin sister.

Yes, the switching-places was all Jessica's idea, so yes, it was her fault.

And yes, Janelle was only trying to help.

No one could really blame her, right?

Unfortunately, every time she asked herself that question, the answer came back: WRONG!

(That was Janelle shouting at herself, not me.)

We arrived at the nursery building and entered. As we approached the little furball, Stephie cooed, "He's sooo cute."

All right, I'll admit it. Maybe he's cute. Just a little. But the little bag of fur also knew how to milk Stephie's heart.

He milked it by the way he perked up his ears and started

meow-ing

"Aw, look at that," Stephie said. (I tried not to.)

He milked it when he bounded up to her and began rubbing against her leg.

"Hi, sweetie," she said. (Oh, brother.)

And he milked it when he began

PURrrrrrrrrr-ing
(Seriously, I think I'm getting sick.)

Janelle looked on. She took a deep breath, and then another. But nothing could untie the knot that kept growing inside her.

"Okay," she said. "Pick him up and let's get this thing over with."

"Yeah!" Stephie said.

Little did they realize that "this thing" wasn't about to be over. In fact, it had barely begun . . .

13

And Worsest

KELE SUDDENLY STOPPED. "Get down," she whispered.

"What?"

"Down!"

Lisa kneeled to join her. "What's going on?"

"The poachers, they're up ahead."

Lisa held her breath and listened. The men weren't talking much now. Mostly just grunting.

"What are they doing?" Lisa asked.

"Piling up the tusks."

The grunting and grumbling continued.

"Sounds like hard work," Lisa said.

"Tusks can be very heavy." Suddenly Kele gasped, "Oh, Lisa . . ."

"What?"

"They've killed two of them!"

"Two?"

"Three!" she blurted. "Counting the one we just saw!"

"Shh," Lisa said.

Kele covered her mouth, trying to stop her tears . . . but the pain was too great.

"How many are there?" Lisa whispered. "How many men do you see?"

Kele counted, "One . . . two . . . three." She sucked in her breath, "Uh-oh."

"Uh-oh?"

"I think they heard us. They're looking our way."

"What do we do?"

"I don't . . ." Kele sounded desperate as she looked around. "Wait! Off to our right, there's a big fig tree. Stay low and follow me." She started crawling away.

"Kele?"

"Shh . . ."

With a heavy sigh, Lisa followed. She always figured being blind had strengthened her in certain ways. But crawling on her hands and knees while hiding from African poachers was not on the list.

"Ouch!" A sharp something jabbed her palm. "What's this?"

"We're in some blood grass," Kele said.

"Blood grass?"

"There's a lot of it here. But it's just a name."

"Tell that to my hand," Lisa said, rubbing it. "Can you see them?" she asked.

"The grass is too high. Just stay low, we're almost there."

Lisa nodded and continued crawling in silence . . . until her other hand landed on a stick that was not only slick . . . but started to wiggle.

"Kele!"

Kele turned back to her.

"Is it . . ." Lisa pointed to the ground, "is that another cobra thing?"

"Nah," Kele said as she turned and continued crawling. "Just a wolf snake."

"And they're not dangerous?"

"Not very."

"*Not* very?"

"Shh," Kele said, "we're almost there."

And she was right. Within a minute they'd crawled out of the weeds and blood grass and had reached the trunk of the giant fig tree.

Just to be sure, Lisa said, "This is a tree, right?"

"What else would it be?"

"It's not some giant animal you haven't told me about . . . or some man-eating plant . . . or some—"

"It's a tree," Kele said. "We can hide here and be perfectly safe."

Lisa took a breath and blew it out. "Perfectly safe" sounded perfectly good to her.

"Except . . ." Kele said as she peered around the tree.

"Except?"

"The men are gone."

"Uh, Kele . . ."

"They completely vanished," Kele said. "Talk about a mystery."

"Um . . ."

"I mean the pile of tusks is still there, but—"

"Kele?"

"What!"

"If we're perfectly safe and there are no animals around . . ."

"Yeah."

"What just grabbed my arm?"

A voice boomed behind them, speaking English: "Hello, ladies."

They jumped and screamed as the man yanked Lisa to her feet.

Another man grabbed Kele, and then a third man joined them.

Well, at least *that* mystery was solved.

Back at home, with Janelle at her side, Stephie was carrying the purring little furball back to his mom. And for the thousandth time all she could say was, "He's sooo cute."

Aren't I cute? And if purrrr-ing was what it took, I could do that. All I had to do was open my mouth and give a warm, little

OOOOOOOOO . . .

Janelle looked to me in surprise. "Winona, are you okay?"
I gave a smile.
"You sound like a ghost."
I gave a frown.
After another breath I tried again.

AAAAAAAAAA . . .

"Winona, you sound sick."
Not exactly the response I wanted. So, I took an even deeper breath and gave it everything I had.

EEEEEEEEEEEE!

To which the little furball in Stephie's arm gave a pathetic

meeeeew . . .

To which Stephie pulled him closer and said, "Winona, please, you're scaring little Bubba."
To which little Bubba stuck his tongue out at me and

Fffffttttt-ed.

Alright, I made up that last part . . . but I'm sure that's what his cunning little kitty brain was thinking. So I suddenly stopped, threw myself on the ground, and started whimpering again.

Janelle looked to Stephie. "Are you sure she's all right?"

Stephie kissed the little fleabag on top of his head and said, "I think Winona's just jealous."

JEALOUS? ME? (I'm not yelling . . . just making a point.)

If I was jealous, why would I just lie there whimpering, expecting her to come back for me? And if I was jealous, why would I stand up and stomp off in the opposite direction to pout? Jealous people don't do that!

Well, okay, maybe jealous *people* do that, but not jealous chimpanzees.

Well, whatever. If Stephie didn't want me hanging around, fine, I wouldn't hang around.

Besides, I had more important things to do . . . like climbing another tree and squeezing in a seven- or eight-hour nap before bedtime.

That's right. If Stephie didn't need me, I didn't need her.

Little did I realize that in a few minutes my best friend would need me more than ever . . .

14

Okay, One More Worst

THE GOOD NEWS WAS LISA AND KELE didn't have to crawl around on their hands and knees anymore.

The bad news was . . . well, just about everything else was bad news:

-getting dragged through the brush by the three men
-getting thrown on the ground beside the elephant tusks
-getting their feet tied so they couldn't run away

Lisa was not impressed by their bad manners. Kele wasn't impressed, either . . . which meant she had to give them a piece of her mind . . . which meant she had to do lots of talking.

"I know why you're wearing those bandanas over your faces. You're afraid we'll recognize you, aren't you? You're not afraid of killing big, defenseless animals, but when it comes to a couple of little kids—"

"We ain't afraid of nothin'," the first man interrupted, speaking English. He turned to the skinny one beside him. "Ain't that right, Kabelo?"

Kabelo winced. "Don't say my name."

"Well, I'm sure not going to call you *Tefo*." He nodded to the other man. "Ain't that right, Tefo?"

Kabelo and Tefo traded looks.

"What?" the first man asked.

"Now she knows *both* of our names," Kabelo said.

The first man shrugged. "Well, at least they don't know my name is Phenyo."

Kabelo and Tefo could only stare. It had been a long time since they'd observed so much emptiness inside one person's head.

"Oops," Phenyo said.

"Oops is right," Kele said. "And don't think we'll forget."

Lisa frowned. "Uh, Kele . . ." she said.

"Just as soon as you let us go, we're running straight to the police to give them your names."

"Kele?"

"They'll know exactly who to arrest."

"Kele!"

"What?"

Lisa started to answer, then realized it was too late.

The men realized it too. (Even Phenyo.)

"Well," Kabelo said as he pulled off his bandana, "I guess we won't be needing these anymore."

The other two agreed and pulled off theirs.

"Ha!" Kele laughed. "Now you're really in trouble!"

"Kele . . ." Lisa whispered.

"Not only do we know your names but now we know exactly what you look—"

"Kele!"

She turned to Lisa and said, "Now what?"

"I don't think you're helping."

"The kid's got a point," Tefo said.

Kabelo nodded. "So what do we do with them?"

Lisa silently prayed that Kele would be able to keep her mouth closed.

"Maybe we just leave 'em here," Phenyo said. "Let the animals eat them."

"A lot you know," Kele said.

The men turned to her.

Lisa prayed harder.

"Wild animals around here try to avoid humans," Kele said. "They don't eat them. At least while they're alive."

"Kele!"

Luckily, they heard an approaching pickup. The sound of metal scraping metal was strangely familiar to Lisa, but she couldn't quite place it. Not yet.

"Ah, there he is now," Kabelo said. He rose to his feet. "Let's get these tusks loaded and get out of here."

"Good," Tefo said. He nodded toward Lisa and Kele. "The boss will know what to do with them."

"That's your boss?" Kele said. "Great, we'll report him, too. You'll all be going to jail!"

Lisa simply dropped her head into her hands.

The pickup appeared, its lights bouncing across their faces until it finally stopped beside them. But it wasn't just any pickup. Now Lisa remembered where she'd heard the sound.

"Daddy!" Kele shouted.

The engine rattled to a stop, and Kele's dad stepped out.

He first looked at his daughter, then to the men. "What's going on?" he demanded.

"These awful people," Kele cried. "We caught them! They're the poachers, Daddy. They're the ones who have been killing the elephants, and me and Lisa caught them red-handed right here where they're waiting for their boss to load up his pickup and . . . and . . ." She frowned, slowing to a stop.

Everyone remained silent. Well, almost everyone.

"I . . . I don't understand," Kele said. "Why were they waiting for you?"

Her dad said nothing.

"She your kid, boss?" Tefo asked the man. "Why was she out here spying on us?"

"We weren't spying," Kele said. "We were . . ." Once again she slowed to a stop. "*Boss*?" She turned to her dad. "He called you . . . *boss*."

Her dad swallowed, then looked to the ground.

"What do we do with them, boss?" Phenyo asked.

"Just . . ." Her dad cleared his throat. "Just load the tusks. I'll take care of—"

"Load up the tusks?" Kele said. "Into *our* pickup?" Her voice started to tremble. "Daddy . . . what's going on?"

"I can explain."

"These men are working for you?"

"Yes, but—"

"They're . . . the poachers."

He knelt to where she and Lisa were still tied. "You have to understand. The herds are growing in number. They're so plentiful now that no one is going to miss—"

"You're the one killing the elephants?"

"Only a few."

"But—"

"We need the money! And as I said—"

"You're a poacher?" Kele's voice grew thin and shaky. "You're . . ." She started to cry.

He reached out to her. "Kele, honey."

She scooted away from him. "No!"

"Please try to understand." He continued stretching out his arms.

"But . . ." Her tears came faster. "You love elephants."

Finally, she let him wrap his arms around her. "Of course I do." He pulled her into an embrace. "But you have to understand—"

Suddenly she stiffened. "No!" She tried pushing him

away. But he held her. "No!" Tears started down her face. She beat him on the back with her fists. "No, no, no . . ."

But he held on until she finally collapsed into his arms, her emotions spent, her body heaving in silent sobs.

15
Seriously Getting Serious

STEPHIE AND I ARE BEST FRIENDS. You can't blame me that we grew up together, or that I used to sneak through the window at night to sleep in her bed. And don't even get me started on how if I beg and whine long enough, she'll find me gooey, half-eaten treats from the wild animal park's garbage cans. (If that's not being best friends, I don't know what is.)

So I decided to ease all her pain and suffering by coming back to join her and that annoying little kitty. (It might have helped if they'd noticed I'd left in the first place.)

Of course, the little fluff brain was still

meeew-ing

and

purrrrr-ing

and doing all those sneaky cute things. But I wasn't worried. In just a few minutes he'd be back with his momma, and I'd have Stephie all to myself.

"Check out Golda," Janelle said as we approached the lion habitat.

We turned to see the big lioness pacing back and forth over the rocks and boulders.

"You think she hears Bubba?" Stephie asked.

"Definitely," Janelle said.

Stephie lifted the cub over her head so Golda could see. "Don't worry, momma! We got your baby right here!"

meeeew . . .

Bubba mewed.

GROWL . . .

Golda growled.

"She sounds serious," Stephie said.

"If it was your kid, wouldn't you be?" Janelle said. "Let's hurry and call her up the ramp into the pen so we can get down there and release him."

We trotted to the back of the habitat where the pen was.

Well, *they* trotted. I would have joined them if buzz-kill Janelle hadn't ordered, "Winona, you stay here. The fewer distractions Golda has the better."

Of course, I had the perfect argument by giving a pathetic little whimper, but Janelle wouldn't listen. Just because I didn't have cute kitty ears, or cute kitty paws, not to mention a cute—I stopped, looked over my shoulder, and checked my rear. Nope. No cute kitty tail, either.

But I did have one thing the little mouse muncher lacked: people skills. So I threw myself on the ground again and cranked up my

whimper . . . whimper-ing

to ultrapathetic.

And Janelle's response?

"Winona, please, you're scaring Bubba."

Insert heavy *SIGH* here . . . (which had no effect, either).

So there I sat watching Stephie and Janelle walk up to the holding pen. Janelle reached over and unlocked the gate. Immediately Golda bounded up the ramp

GROWL-ing

and trying to paw through the bars to her.

"It's okay," Stephie said. She did her best to comfort Golda by

CLICK-ing . . . **CLOCK**-ing . . .

and

CLACK-ing

her tongue like Lisa had taught her. But momma cat was not in the mood. (And, just between you and me, Stephie wasn't that great of a clicker, clocker, or clacker.)

"Okay," Janelle finally said. "I'm going to open the gate. Move around to the back of the pen with Bubba, so she'll run inside and try to get you."

Stephie nodded and carried Bubba around to the back as Janelle counted, "Three . . . two . . . one!"

She unlatched the gate and Golda raced into the pen— leaping, growling, and snarling as she tried to swat at Stephie who was safe on the other side of the bars. Janelle slammed the gate shut. Now Golda was locked in the holding pen,

GROWLING . . . snarling

and pacing more than ever.

"Okay," Janelle said. "Let's climb down into the habitat and release Bubba. Then we'll come back up and open the gate so they'll finally be together."

Stephie moved to the ladder. Holding Bubba in one arm, she climbed down. "Hear that, little fella?" she said. "You're finally getting back with your momma."

Janelle followed right behind. But they'd barely reached

the floor of the habitat with its stones and boulders before Janelle's phone rang.

Janelle saw it was Jessica and picked up. "How's it going?" she asked.

"I need you here!" Jessica whispered.

"What are you talking about? Mom's there."

"Not anymore."

"What?"

"Hector got in another fight with those kids."

"What's that got to do with—"

"She's over at the office."

"She's not in the auditorium?"

"Which is why you can come."

"Jess, I'm not—"

"This is the last time. I promise."

Janelle closed her eyes.

Jessica continued. "If you don't come, we'll both get busted for sure."

Janelle looked up to the pen where Golda was

GROWLING, yowling

and pacing.

"Janelle?"

"Look," she said. "Stephie and I are reuniting Golda with her cub."

"Do that when we're done. This won't take long. You and Steph can do that when you get back."

"And how do you suggest I get there?"

"Take the bike."

"It's three miles away."

"Which is why you have to hurry."

"Jess—"

"I can stall Mrs. Crawly a little, but you have to come *now*!"

Janelle swallowed. She looked back up to Golda.

"Janelle?"

Then she looked over to Stephie, who stood by the little pond ready to set Bubba down.

"*Janelle*." One thing you could say about Jessica, she never gives up. "*Janelle!*" (See what I mean?)

Janelle took a deep breath. "All right," she said, "but this is the very last time."

"Absolutely. Now hurry!" Before Janelle could answer, Jessica disconnected.

Stephie called over to her, "What's going on?"

"Change of plans," Janelle said. "We'll do this later."

"But—"

"I'm sorry, Steph."

"*Janelle!*"

"I promise, we'll do this as soon as I get back. You've got my word."

But, Janelle asked herself, with all the lying she'd been doing lately, was her word worth anything anymore?

16
Loads of Lies

BACK IN BOTSWANA, KELE'S DAD WAS STILL TRYING to untangle his own mess. "It's not what it looks like," he kept saying. "Sweetheart, listen to me . . . listen."

Kele took a ragged breath and managed to stop crying . . . at least for the moment.

"Here." Her dad pulled a knife from his pocket and began cutting the tape holding her feet. "Let's get rid of this."

Kele sniffed. "What do you mean, 'It's not what it looks like'?"

He glanced over to the men, then lowered his voice so they couldn't hear. "I'm not a poacher, I'm . . . like a spy."

Kele wiped her eyes. "A spy?"

"I'm undercover. I'm pretending to work with them so I can find who the real poachers are."

"But those men," she looked over to the truck where they were loading the tusks, "they called you 'boss.'"

"Shh . . . I know, I know. They're in on it too."

"Then why are you whispering? And they killed those elephants. We heard the gunshots. We saw them. And now they're taking the tusks." She hesitated. "Now *you're* taking the tusks."

"That's right. To find the buyer. We had to sacrifice a few of the animals to find who is in charge of the much bigger operation."

"So you're actually trying to help these men?"

"Yes, of course. That's why Dr. Mooketsi hired me." He reached out and Kele let him pull her into another hug.

There was something in his voice that Lisa didn't trust. She couldn't put her finger on it—maybe it was the catch in his throat, or how far-fetched the story sounded. Either way, something wasn't right.

Janelle pedaled faster . . . and wheezed harder. She was no jock, that was for sure. Not like her sister. And riding bikes was not her thing. (Actually, anything involving sweating was not her thing.) Her legs already started to ache.

But time was running out. She'd told Stephie to take Bubba back to the nursery. She promised they'd bring him to Golda just as soon as she got back. Stephie wasn't thrilled with the idea, but she had no choice.

Janelle pedaled harder. She had to get to the school on time. But she pedaled harder for another reason.

How had it begun? It was just a clever little thing Jessica dreamed up.

She bore down on the pedals. Her legs ached worse. It was getting hard to catch her breath.

It was just one little lie. But it kept growing . . . and growing . . . and growing. And with it, an impossible weight was growing inside her chest.

"The LORD detests lying lips . . ."

She pedaled even harder—sucking air, feeling it burn the back of her throat. But she wouldn't stop. She couldn't stop. She wasn't afraid of getting caught—well, there was that—but . . .

"The LORD detests lying lips . . ."

If she pedaled fast enough, hard enough, maybe she could make the guilt go away. At least that's what she hoped. But somehow she knew even that was a lie.

The fire in her throat spread into her lungs. Her legs began cramping. She was gasping for air.

Just a lie. Everyone lies.

"The LORD detests lying lips . . ."

The road in front of her blurred. She wiped her eyes, but it did no good. They just kept filling with tears.

Stephie and I carried Bubba halfway back to the nursery when we stopped. I hoped it was for a nice belly-rub, which I'd not had all afternoon thanks to that spoiled little purring machine. Or maybe we were going to search for goodies in one of the park's garbage cans. But my super chimp brain soon realized it was something else. (The fact that Stephie turned to me and explained what it was she was thinking also helped.)

"Wait . . . what are we doing here?" she said. "We don't need Janelle. Golda's still up in her pen. I'll just take Bubba back down into the habitat and then climb up to open her pen myself. That'll show everyone."

It made perfect sense to me. The sooner we dumped baby Bubba, the sooner Stephie could get back to my favorite subject . . . me.

So we turned and headed back to the lion exhibit.

Now everyone was happy.

Well, everyone but Golda. When she saw us return, she started

GROWLING

and this time added a mighty

ROAR

so loud that it made the fur on my neck rise. Of course, I immediately reached up and took Stephie's hand. Poor kid. I bet she was terrified. It got even scarier when Golda

ROAR-ed!

even louder—which is why I squeezed Stephie's hand harder.

"Don't worry," she said. "Golda's just mad because she thinks we're teasing her with Bubba again." She turned and shouted up to the pen, "It's okay, momma. Be patient. We're really going to do it this time!"

If Golda had heard that, she did a pretty good job of pretending she hadn't. You could tell by the way she paced back and forth. And as we approached, she leaped at us against the bars so hard that the whole pen shook. And if we had any doubts she threw in an extra-loud

ROAR

that was terrifying in the I'm-glad-I'm-not-wearing-pants-because-I-might-have-to-change-them kind of way.

When we reached the ladder to go down into the habitat, Stephie turned to me and said, "Winona, you stay up here."

I nodded, figuring it was the least I could do. What I kind of wanted to do was run to the house, crawl under a bed, and dial 911 (which never works because my fingers are too fat and none of the dispatchers have bothered to learn to speak Chimpish). Still, as Stephie's best friend, I agreed to staying up here and staying alive instead of going inside the habitat, where I might not keep living.

Stephie held Bubba close as she climbed down the ladder into the habitat. She crossed over to the edge of the pond and set him down. "Wait right here, little buddy. We're going to let mom in."

Of course, Bubba looked back up to her with those disgustingly cute little eyes and gave his disgustingly cute little

meeew . . .

and, of course, Stephie had to reach down and give him one last pat on the head.

Then she turned and started back up the ladder. Once there, she crossed to Golda's pen where the big cat paced harder and added a couple, even louder

ROARs

just to make things interesting.

Stephie reached for the latch on the gate, careful to avoid Golda's slapping paws . . . which were too big to get through the bars, but big enough to mean business. Opening the latch, Stephie was about to slide open the gate when she heard Bubba. But instead of his usual *meewing* thing, he was

HOWL-ing.

She looked down into the habitat to see the clumsy cub had fallen into the habitat's pond. Not only fallen, but by the way he was thrashing about, it looked like he was drowning!

17
The Truth Surfaces

HOW COULD LISA EXPLAIN TO KELE that her father was lying? Not only was his story hard to believe, she could hear the deception in his voice. And she heard it in Kele's voice too . . . the way she was trying so hard to believe him. But then Lisa heard something else: the crack of twigs, the rustling of grass, and then a voice:

"What's going on here?" It was Dr. Mooketsi. "Kele?" he shouted. Then he called to Kele's father, "Oteng? What's going on?"

"Dr. Mooketsi!" Kele's father answered in surprise.

Then Lisa heard another voice: "Lisa?"

Her heart leaped and she shouted, "Dad! Over here!"

"What on earth?"

And then she heard a third voice. "What'd you do this time, sis?"

"Nick!"

The two ran to join her as Dr. Mooketsi repeated, "What's going on?"

"I've . . . I've caught these men," Kele's father answered. "These are the poachers!"

"What?" one of the men called from the pickup. "What are you saying?"

"It's too late," Kele's father shouted back at him. "We caught you red-handed."

"Daddy?" There was no missing Kele's confusion.

"You hired us!" another one of the men shouted. "We work for *you*!"

"Right." Kele's father forced a laugh. "Like I would hire you."

"Oteng," Dr. Mooketsi said. "What are they talking about?"

As Kele's father tried to explain, Dad knelt down to Lisa. "Sweetheart, are you okay?"

"Yeah," she said.

"Nick," Dad said, "you still got your pocketknife?"

"Right here."

"Give it to me."

Nick passed him the knife, and Dad began cutting the tape off Lisa's feet.

"Oteng!" Dr. Mooketsi demanded.

"You have to understand," Kele's father answered. "It was the only way I could ever catch them."

"I never authorized this!" Dr. Mooketsi said. "And why are they loading the tusks into *your* truck?"

"Daddy . . ." Kele's voice cracked.

"Not now, honey."

But of course Kele didn't know how to stop talking. "You said Dr. Mooketsi hired you to help the poachers."

"I said that?" Her father gave a nervous chuckle. "Why would I say that?"

"Let's get out of here!" one of the men shouted.

Lisa heard them scramble into the truck.

"Stop right there!" Dr. Mooketsi yelled.

Lisa heard the engine start up.

"Wait for me!" Kele's father shouted and began running to them.

"Oteng!" Dr. Mooketsi yelled after him.

Kele called, "Daddy!"

"Hurry!" the men shouted as the truck's engine revved.

He was nearly there.

"Daddy!" Kele cried.

Something in his daughter's voice made him slow.

The men shouted, "Let's go!"

"Daddy . . ."

Finally, he came to a stop.

"What are you doing?" they yelled.

"Daddy . . ."

The truck revved louder. "Get in!"

But Kele's father stood frozen, unable to move.

"Fine!" one of the men shouted. "Have it your way!"

Lisa heard the gears grind and the truck leap forward.

"You're a fool, Oteng!" one of the men shouted as they sped off. "A fool!" another yelled as they disappeared into the night.

Lisa heard Kele running to her father. She heard her crying as she fell into his arms and buried her face into his chest.

"I'm sorry, honey." Her father could barely choke out the words as he held her. "I'm so . . . sorry."

Janelle pedaled so hard that by the time she got to the school her legs felt like spaghetti. And the worst thing about having spaghetti legs is finding the strength to hit the brakes and stop. And the worst thing about that is . . .

K-thunk

Ow!

. . . running into the bike rack.

But at least she was there. Now all she had to do was run to the auditorium. Well, she couldn't exactly run yet . . .

"Come on, legs," she ordered, "work with me, here." It took some coaxing: "Take a step . . . come on now. All right! And now another. There, I knew you could do it! And another . . ." until she finally arrived.

She hobbled into the lobby, threw open the auditorium doors . . . and froze.

The spelling bee had already started. Jessica stood on stage in line with the other contestants looking as nervous as . . . well, as nervous as someone about to get busted for telling loads of lies.

The good news was Mom wasn't there. Actually, other than Mrs. Crawly, no one was there, which gives you an idea about how much people cared about this event. But Mom was different. She always showed up for her kids . . . except right now she had to show up in the principal's office to deal with Hector's latest fight.

Janelle gently closed the doors and limped around the lobby to the back of the stage. Once she arrived, she saw Chloe standing in the wings.

"Good," Chloe whispered, "I thought you'd never get here."

She turned toward the stage and waved to Jessica. But Jessica was focused on Mrs. Crawly who was saying, "And now, Jessica, are you ready for your next word?"

Chloe tried getting Jessica's attention again, this time throwing in a loud

psssssssssst . . .

That did the trick. Jessica turned and saw both girls standing in the wings.

"Jessica?" Mrs. Crawly called to her. "Is there a problem?"

"Uh, no, ma'am."

"Bathroom," Chloe hissed. "Tell her you have to use the bathroom." (Of course, it was another lie, but by now who was counting.)

Jessica glanced at Chloe, then turned to Mrs. Crawly. "I need a bathroom break."

"Certainly," Mrs. Crawly said. "But hurry."

Jessica nodded and headed backstage.

When she arrived Chloe whispered, "Your mom still isn't here."

"I know," Jessica said.

"So, hurry! Change clothes!"

"Right," Jessica said. She started to peel off her sweater.

"Guys," Janelle protested. "What if Mom—"

Chloe interrupted. "I'm not giving up the chance to have no homework for a week. Hurry."

With a heavy sigh, Janelle unbuttoned her shirt. Not only were they lying, but now they'd joined forces with Chloe . . . the very last person they liked or trusted. Then again, Janelle thought, maybe there wasn't that much difference between them. Not anymore.

Once they finished changing, Chloe whispered, "Okay. Go, go!"

With a deep breath . . . and promising she'd never do it again (just like all the other times) Janelle started forward.

"Wait!" Jessica whispered. "Your glasses."

Janelle pulled them off and tossed them to Jessica.

"Go!" Chloe whispered.

She stepped onstage to take Jessica's place in line. But not before a little

bump . . . stumble.

"Hey," a student complained.
And another

bump, trip.

"Watch where you're going," another grumbled.
When she finally found her place, Mrs. Crawly asked, "Are we ready, Jessica?"
Janelle nodded as she shielded her eyes from the light.
"Your word is . . . *perjurer.*"
She took another breath. *This is it,* she told herself. *One last lie and it will all be over.*
"Jessica?"
Janelle swallowed and began. "Perjurer. P-e-r-j-u—"
"Janelle?" another voice interrupted. And it wasn't Mrs. Crawly's voice. "What are you doing up there?"
Squinting into the light, she half croaked, "Mom!?"
"Where's Jessica? And where are your glasses?"
Janelle closed her eyes. She felt her face growing hot.
"Jessica?" Mom called. "Jessica, are you here? Jessica!"
Slowly, Jessica stepped out onto the stage.
"What's going on?" Mrs. Crawly demanded.
"I can explain," Jessica said.

Both women waited.

Jessica cleared her throat. "I . . . that is, we . . . I mean, um—"

"It was all a big lie!" Chloe shouted as she ran onto the stage. "I just found out about these two switching places. They've been lying from the very start."

The twins traded looks. (*Good ol' Chloe.*)

"Of course, I tried to stop them," Chloe continued. "I mean, what a terrible mark this is against our class, right, Mrs. Crawly? And Mrs. Mulligan, I can't imagine how embarrassed you must be. I know *I* would be. That's why I told them . . ."

Janelle couldn't remember much of what happened after that—just the sick, sinking feeling in her stomach. But she felt something else as well. A type of relief . . . like someone had taken a huge weight off her shoulders. Sure, the two of them would be punished. And sure, it might not be any fun. But now, at last, it was finally over.

Well, not exactly.

Because Janelle Mulligan was about to discover that lying can cause even greater problems than just getting caught and being punished . . .

18

More Truth

ONCE DAD AND DR. MOOKETSI MADE SURE Lisa and Kele were safe, they began the long walk back to their camp. Even with Nick's and Kele's talents as nonstop talkers, it was strangely quiet. And Kele's father? He didn't say a word. What could he say? He'd been found out, and no amount of fast-talking or lying could save him.

Dr. Mooketsi only broke the silence once when he turned to him and said, "You know there will be consequences. *Serious* consequences."

"Yes, sir," Kele's father answered. "I understand."

Back in Mom's car, the silence was exactly the same. Janelle and Jessica were totally wrong and totally busted. Mom never said much when she was angry. No yelling, no shouting, just nerve-racking silence.

But she did say one thing: "You know there will be consequences."

"Yes, ma'am," they mumbled.

"*Serious* consequences."

And back at the animal park? With Bubba busy trying not to drown, there was only one thing Stephie could do. She leaped from Golda's pen and raced down the ladder to save him.

Actually, there was one other thing she could have done . . . locked the gate to Golda's pen *SO SHE COULDN'T GET OUT!*

(Yup, I'm shouting here.)

"Hang on, Bubba," she yelled as she raced down the ladder and ran over to the pond.

Of course, Golda saw the whole thing from her pen. So you really can't blame her for slapping and pawing at the gate until it opened.

And you can't blame Stephie for being so busy wading into the pond and scooping up the soggy furball that she didn't notice. "It's okay, sweetie," she kept saying. "I've got you now, everything's okay."

And she would have been right except for Golda's

ROAR!

When Stephie spun around, she saw the lioness racing down the ramp into the habitat and straight to the water's edge—snarling and ready to attack!

"H-hi, Golda," she stuttered. "You want your baby? I've got him right h-here."

But the big lion wanted more than her baby. She wanted Stephie, too . . . in a *Rated R for Violence* kind of way.

Of course, I wanted to jump down there and help. But I have this allergy, you see. I'm allergic to being eaten alive by lions. I would break into a bad case of death every time it happens. So I resorted to my tried and true:

OO-oo Ah-ah EE-ee! OO-oo Ah-ah EE-ee! OO-oo Ah-ah EE-ee!

(Okay, so I was a little excited.)

So was Golda. But not over me. Just Bubba.

And Stephie.

"It's okay, girl," Stephie tried to explain. "Just let me get to shore so I can hand him over to you."

But Golda wasn't interested in explanations—just pacing at the water's edge, snarling, and

ROAR-ing.

"I can't put him back in the water," Stephie said. "He'll drown. You have to let me get him to shore!"

She took another step toward shore but was slowed by Golda's rather rude

SNAAAARL . . . GROOOWL.

"Nice Golda," she said. "See, I'm not hurting him. I'm just trying to—"

GROOOWL . . . SNAAAARL . . .

Stephie stopped. What could she do? She looked around. Why hadn't she waited for Janelle to come back? Why did she have to prove to everybody she could do this by herself? Why—

Suddenly, an idea popped into her head. Holding Bubba in one hand, she reached into her pocket and pulled out her phone.

She hit Janelle's number . . . and waited.

19

Joining Forces!

BACK INSIDE MOM'S CAR, JANELLE PICKED UP her phone on the first ring. "Hello?"

"If that's one of your friends," Mom said, "tell her your phone privileges are suspended until—"

"It's Stephie!" Janelle cried. "She's in the lion habitat with Golda!"

"She's what!?"

"I'm putting her on speakerphone."

"Stephie?" Mom called. "Sweetie, are you all right?"

"I am for now. But Golda's kind of mad, and I'm kind of stuck in the habitat with her."

"You're in the—" Mom was interrupted by another one of Golda's

ROARs

"Stephie!" she shouted.

"What do I do?" Stephie sounded scared. Really scared. "She's got me trapped, and she's really mad."

"Talk to her," Mom said. "Try to calm her."

"She thinks I'm going to hurt Bubba."

As the two spoke, Janelle's mind raced. First came the guilt. None of this would have happened if she hadn't gotten involved in the spelling bee deception and if she'd stayed with Stephie. Then, suddenly, an idea surfaced.

"Stephie," she said. "Remember the tongue clicking Lisa taught you. The one she uses to calm Golda?"

"I can't—"

"Stephie—"

Her voice was shaking. "I'm scared."

"Try it!"

Back in the habitat, Golda stepped into the water then stepped out. She wanted to save Bubba, to attack Stephie, but she wasn't sure how to do it while swimming. Like many cats, big or small, she was afraid of water.

Janelle pleaded through Stephie's phone. "Just try it. Like Lisa taught you."

Stephie nodded and took a shaky breath. "Nice Golda." Her voice trembled. Her mouth was like cotton. "Good

Golda." She tried clicking her tongue, but her mouth was too dry. Nothing close to the sound came out. She tried again. Still nothing.

"I can't!" she cried. "Not like Lisa!" She watched as Golda stepped into the water again. "If Lisa was here, she could do it, but I can't!"

Back in the car, Stephie's words gave Janelle an idea. "Mom, what's the code for Lisa?"

"Code?"

"When we call Dad, what's the calling code?"

Mom thought a moment then answered, "267. Why?"

Janelle spoke back into the phone. "Stephie, hang on." She punched the code into her phone followed by Lisa's number. It took a moment to get through, but finally . . .

Lisa's phone rang just as they arrived back at the campsite. She pulled it from her pocket and barely answered before Janelle interrupted.

"Lisa!"

Lisa frowned. "Janelle? What are you doing calling—"

"We've got a problem!"

Back in the habitat, Golda was now in the water. She was still pacing, not swimming. Not yet. But every moment she was getting closer to trying.

"Janelle?" Stephie cried.

At first there was no answer.

"Janelle!"

And then her voice came back on. "Steph, I've got Lisa here on a conference call. Lisa, are you there?"

"Right here," Lisa said. "Stephie?"

"Lisa," she said. "I'm scared!"

"No worries. Is Golda there?"

"She's getting ready to attack!"

"Okay. I want you to put your phone on *speakerphone*."

"I don't understand."

"Just . . . trust me."

Stephie pulled the phone from her face and tapped the speakerphone setting.

"Are we good?" Lisa asked.

"Yes."

"Now point it toward Golda."

Stephie raised the phone and aimed it at the lion.

"Alright," Lisa said. She cleared her throat. Then, trying to sound calm, she called, "Hey, Golda? Hey, girl. It's me, Lisa. How are you?"

Golda gave a little

GROOOWL

and continued pacing.

"Yeah, I hear that," Lisa said. "But Stephie here, she's trying to help. Bubba's going to be okay. I promise. But you've got to trust her."

Golda kept pacing.

"Golda? Girl?" Lisa repeated. "It's me, Lisa."

Golda finally slowed and stared at the phone, cocking her head.

"She hears you," Stephie said. "She recognizes your voice."

"Good," Lisa said. "Good. Keep pointing the phone at her."

"I am."

And then Lisa started to

Click, click, click

her tongue with that special way only she could do.

At first nothing happened. But as Lisa continued, Golda slowly came to a stop.

"It's working!" Stephie cried. She held the phone out further.

"Great," Lisa said and continued

Click, click, click-ing

Golda cocked her head again.

"Now what do I do?" Stephie asked.

Lisa kept clicking as Janelle answered. "Get out of the water. But as far from Golda as possible. Put Bubba on the shore and get out of there."

Stephie nodded and sloshed toward the far bank. But as she moved, Golda followed her.

"She's following me!" she cried. "What do I do?"

No one had an answer.

"I'll put him down," she said. "When I get to the shore, I'll put him down and run."

"No!" everyone shouted. "Don't run!"

"What am I supposed to do?"

No one had a clue . . .

Except me! That was my best friend down there. She was totally trapped, about to become Kitty Cat Chow! Even though it went against everything I believed in—like being strong, courageous, and not dying—I leaped off the wall and down into the habitat.

Super Chimp to the rescue! (And probably to the funeral home too.)

Having no idea what to do, I shouted out

00-oo Ah-ah EE-ee

to distract Golda. It worked perfectly . . . except for the part that made it worse (which was all of it). The truth is, it seemed to make Golda even angrier. She waded deeper into the water.

"Janelle!" Stephie cried, "she's coming closer. Lisa!"

And then, without thinking (one of my specialties) I raced toward Stephie, splashing into the pond. Before she could stop me, I reached up and grabbed the soggy furball from her.

The good news was I had him in my arms. The bad news was Golda finally decided to swim. Toward me!

"Winona!" Stephie cried.

I had no time to explain (or make out a will). All I could do was swim while Golda was gaining on me every second.

I heard Stephie yelling, along with everyone in Mom's car

and the rest of the family in Africa. It was going to be close, but I had to reach the far wall and scramble up it.

I heard Golda splashing, then felt her hot breath on my back.

She reached out and nearly got me.

I swam harder until . . .

I finally reached the wall.

Using my vast athletic skills, I quickly climbed to safety, although Golda raked a giant paw across my rear—kind of a going-away present.

Once I reached the top of the wall, I looked across the habitat and saw Stephie climbing the ladder out of danger.

Whew, I did it! I don't know how, but I did it.

(Score: Chimps 1, Lions 0.)

So there I stood, victorious, grateful to be alive, and planning what type of celebration dinner they'd throw in my honor. (I wouldn't be too picky, so long as little Julie didn't do the cooking.)

And then I heard:

meeeew

I looked down and saw the furball shivering in my arms. He was obviously cold. I pulled him in closer, letting him burrow deeper into my chest to get warm. Then, to make matters worse, the kitty con artist started to

purrr

He began rubbing his face against me.

Knock it off, you little furball. You're not fooling any—

purrrrr

Well, okay, maybe a little scratch behind the ears. But that's all you're getting from—

purrrrrrrrrr

Okay, fine. And a little scratching under the chin, but that's—

PURRRRRRRRRR . . .

Hmm . . . he *is* kind of cute.

20
Wrapping Up

LISA, NICK, AND DAD WOULDN'T BE HOME for another week, so Mom decided to set up something called a video call. I'm not sure how this human magic works, but it meant we all sat on the sofa in front of a computer screen. And over in Africa, Nick and Dad sat in front of their own screen . . . with Lisa and the baby elephant in the back.

After the usual

"How are you guys?" "Qeeo, Ah-ah, EE-ee."
"Hi, Dad! "Miss you!", "Is that baby Thato?"
"Are you really in Africa?" "Hi, Lisa." "Hi, Daddy!" "When you coming home?"

we got down to business.

"So where is Hector?" Dad asked as he peered into his screen.

"He's doing schoolwork," Stephie said.

"No kidding? Since when does he like schoolwork?"

"Actually," Mom explained, "he's doing work *at* school. I convinced Principal Corning the best discipline would be for him to pick up trash with the boys he'd fought."

"Smart," Dad said.

Mom adjusted baby Al on her lap and grinned at all of us. "You have to be smart when you're running a small city."

"And the twins?" Dad asked.

"Over here," Janelle groaned, trying to raise her arm.

"You sound in pain."

"Coach Buffton thought extra pull-ups would help make up for the classes I missed. Plus push-ups, plus sit-ups, plus anything else she can think of."

Mom added, "Not to mention the extra chores I've given her and Jessica to do around the park."

"Where is Jess?" Dad asked.

"Upstairs doing homework," Janelle said. "Lots of it."

"I'm guessing for English?"

"Mrs. Crawly thinks a lot like Coach Buffton."

"Hi, Daddy," Julie chirped from beside Mom.

"Hi, sweetie," Dad said. "Are you doing anymore cooking?"

"Yes. I've got lots more ideas."

"That's great."

"But Mom says I have to wait until you and Nick get back to enjoy them."

"Don't wait on my account," Nick said. "Plenty of tasty food over here."

"Not as good as my chocolate scrambled eggs," Julie said.

Nick gave an uneasy swallow.

"With mustard!" she added.

Even on the computer screen he looked a little pale.

"How's Bubba?" Lisa asked from where she stood behind Nick and Dad.

"Safe and sound with Golda," Stephie said. "Me and Janelle did that this morning."

"Oo-oo Ah-ah EE-ee," I said.

Stephie reached over and gave me a much-earned head scratch. "Winona too."

"And the baby elephant?" Mom asked. "How's Thato?"

Dad and Nick leaned to the side so we could see him standing next to Lisa. "His appetite has come back," she said. "And he's starting to drink." She snapped her fingers over a bucket of water and he obediently dropped in his trunk, sucking it up.

"Wow," Janelle said, "he's really thirsty."

"They don't drink with their trunks," Lisa said. "Just hold water in them. Up to two and a half gallons."

Dad added, "Lisa and her new friend, Kele, have spent a lot of time with Thato, and he has learned to trust them. Soon we'll introduce him to a new herd."

"Yeah," Nick said. "And between him, his smell, and all these flies, it won't be soon enough."

"Nick," Lisa chided.

"All I'm saying is we've spent enough time over one stupid animal."

"He's not stupid," Lisa argued.

As if proving her point, Thato raised his trunk high over his head.

"Right," Nick said. "Well, if he's so smart maybe he could—"

Suddenly Thato shot the water out of his trunk . . . directly onto Nick!

"Hey!" Nick shouted, coughing and choking. "Hey! Hey!"

We all laughed as the water kept coming.

But since Nick was sitting at the computer, it was also getting drenched.

The picture began to freeze and flicker as Dad shouted: "I think . . . we're . . . losing . . ."

It got worse until it was clear the call was ending:

". . . love . . . you guys . . ."

We all shouted back,

"I love you!" "See you soon." "I love you too." "Tell Thato hi." "Be safe." "Hurry home." "I miss you." "Bring me back something." "I'll tell Bubba hi." "OO-oo, Ah-ah-EE-ee." "Bye-bye—" "I'll cook you a nice surprise!"

And then they were gone.

But not for long. They'd be home soon. And we'd all be together again . . . fighting, laughing . . . and learning to love each other despite our differences. Because that's how it is with us.

That's how it is with the magnificent Mulligans.

Thoughts and Questions

From The Magnificent Mulligans creator, Bill Myers

Chapter 1

1. Nick likes to brag. Isn't it interesting how many times it gets him into trouble or makes him look foolish? Consider this verse from God's Word: *"Let another praise you, and not your own mouth; a stranger, and not your own lips" (Proverbs 27:2)*. What does this say about God's opinion of boasting?

2. Lisa is afraid of flying. What are you afraid of? How can the following verse help? *"Fear not, for I am with you; be not dismayed, for I am your God; I will strengthen you, I will help you, I will uphold you with my righteous right hand" (Isaiah 41:10)*.

Chapter 2

1. Have you ever had someone tempt you to do something you knew was wrong? What did you do?

2. Read Matthew 4:1-11. What did Jesus do when Satan tried to tempt Him in the wilderness?

Chapter 3

1. Have you ever told one lie to cover up another lie? What do we observe about lying once the lies start adding up?
2. If people found out you lied, how would it affect their trust in you in the future? How does this line up with Proverbs 22:1: *"A good name is to be chosen rather than great riches, and favor is better than silver or gold"*?

Chapter 4

1. Read Galatians 6:7-8. How would you explain these two verses in your own words?
2. Nick spends a lot of time reaping what he has sown. What does that mean in the context of this chapter? Have you experienced a situation in which you reaped what you've sown?

Chapter 5

1. Even though Jessica and Janelle succeeded for a while at being dishonest, how did it cost them emotionally?
2. Do you think it affected their relationship with God? In your own experience, how has lying or committing other sins affected your relationship with God?

Chapter 6

1. The guilt is piling up in Janelle's heart. What could she do to remove it? How would this verse apply to Janelle's situation: *"If we confess our sins, he is faithful and just to forgive us our sins and to cleanse us from all unrighteousness" (1 John 1:9)*?

2. How can God's promise to forgive sin and cleanse your heart influence your life today?

Chapter 7

1. Why is Hector avoiding Mom and Dad? When you do something wrong, do you try to avoid your parents?

2. Many people also try to avoid God when they sin. Read Ecclesiastes 12:14 and Proverbs 15:3. Can we ever really avoid God?

Chapter 8

1. Janelle turned to the Bible for help, although at the time it didn't exactly make her feel better. Can you think of times in your life when God's truth might have hurt for a moment but was better for you in the long run?

2. How does this verse apply to Janelle's predicament: *"For the moment all discipline seems painful rather than pleasant, but later it yields the peaceful fruit of righteousness to those who have been trained by it" (Hebrews 12:11)*?

Chapter 9

1. Look at Proverbs 13:21: *"Disaster pursues sinners, but the righteous are rewarded with good."* What do you think it means that "disaster pursues sinners"? Do you get the feeling that disaster is about to catch up with Jessica and Janelle? If so, why?
2. Like any sin, telling lies can seem good for a while—like helping to get us out of trouble! But eventually the price has to be paid, and the cost is often worse than the trouble the lie tried to avoid. Can you think of a situation from your life where a lie that was intended to help you avoid trouble actually caused *more* trouble?

Chapter 10

1. Have you noticed how the twins' deceptions keep growing and growing? Do you think the twins' consequences would be less severe if they had admitted their first lie, without the constant covering up?

Chapter 11

1. Kele and Lisa are doing their own brand of deception and disobedience by sneaking off after dark to be near the hippos. And now they may have to pay their own harsh price. Instead of trying to stop the poachers themselves, what could they have done instead?

Chapter 12

1. Guilt continues piling up in Janelle's heart. Do you think there is anything about her sin that she is enjoying now? How about Jessica? Is she enjoying the outcome of the two sisters' great lie?

2. Here's what David had to say when he tried to hide and keep his sin silent: *"For when I kept silent, my bones wasted away through my groaning all day long" (Psalm 32:3).* Is something like that happening to Janelle?

Chapter 13

1. Winona seems jealous of the attention that Bubba the lion cub is getting from Stephie. What does it mean to be "jealous" or "envious"? What does the following verse tell us about the connection between love and envy? *"Love is patient and kind; love does not envy or boast; it is not arrogant" (1 Corinthians 13:4).*

2. When God gave us the Ten Commandments, He told us not to create and worship idols. *"For I the LORD your God am a jealous God,"* He announced (Exodus 20:5). How is God's love and jealousy for us different from Winona's selfish jealousy?

Chapter 14

1. Can sin do more than just hurt the person who is sinning? Can you think of an example?

2. How is Kele's father's lie hurting their relationship?

Chapter 15

1. As Jessica and Janelle's great lie keeps growing, the twins are no longer in charge. Instead of using lies to get their way, now the lies are using them. Can you think of other sins that start off small but grow to take over people's lives?

Chapter 16

1. Stephie is trying too hard to prove herself to others. Instead of racing ahead and trying to release Bubba on her own, what should she have done?
2. Can you think of a time when you wanted to prove yourself so much that you disobeyed your parents or other authority? What happened?

Chapters 17 and 18

1. The twins were finally caught, and Kele's father had to admit to his lie about being the leader of the elephant poachers. It's painful to get caught, but there is something good about it too. What is that good part? Have you ever experienced that?
2. Consider James 5:16: *"Therefore, confess your sins to one another and pray for one another, that you may be*

healed." In the long run, which feels better—to keep sinning or to confess our sins to others and to God so we become clean?

Here is another important part of confession: *"If we confess our sins, he is faithful and just to forgive us our sins and to cleanse us from all unrighteousness" (1 John 1:9).* Not just some unrighteousness, but ALL!

Chapter 19

1. Even though they're so different from each other, and they often make mistakes, the Mulligans always come together to help each other. Can you think of a time you were there to help someone even though they were different from you or they made mistakes?
2. Jesus did that a lot—helping people who were different or who made mistakes. Can you recall a few times when He helped people who were different from Him and who were known to be sinners?

Chapter 20

1. What lessons stood out most to you in this story?
2. Which lessons do you hope to apply in your own life?